GUT SHOT!

Clint opened his eyes just moments before some-one started banging on the door. He drew his gun from the holster just as the door slammed open.

The first man through the door had a gun in his hand. Clint didn't need to know anything more. He fired once, catching the man in the chest. The impact of the bullet drove the man back, knocking him into a second man right behind him.

Clint fired again. As his bullet struck the second man in the belly, the man discharged his own gun into the ceiling, then fell to the floor, doubled over, clutching his belly.

"Nobody can save you now, friend," Clint said. "You're gut shot and you're going to die. Talk while you have the chance. Who sent you after me?"

But the man didn't answer. He whimpered, and blubbered, and then blood bubbles appeared in his lips. Moments later, he was dead.

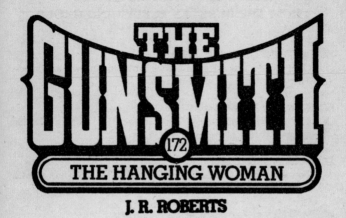

THE GUNSMITH

172

THE HANGING WOMAN

J. R. ROBERTS

JOVE BOOKS, NEW YORK

THE HANGING WOMAN

A Jove Book / published by arrangement with
the author

PRINTING HISTORY
Jove edition / April 1996

The Putnam Berkley World Wide Web site address is
http://www.berkley.com

ISBN: 0-515-11844-3

A JOVE BOOK®
Jove Books are published by The Berkley Publishing Group,
200 Madison Avenue, New York, New York 10016.
JOVE and the "J" design are trademarks
belonging to Jove Publications, Inc.

PRINTED IN THE UNITED STATES OF AMERICA

10 9 8 7 6 5 4 3 2 1

THE HANGING WOMAN

ONE

Clint could see from a distance that something was hanging from the tree. He hoped that it wasn't what he thought it was, but as he got closer he could see that it surely was.

A body.

He was in Arizona, fifty miles from the nearest town, and had stumbled across the result of what had to have been a lynching. The only other possibility was suicide, and he could think of better ways to do that than a broken neck or—if things went wrong—slow strangulation.

The tree was on a hill, which was why he was able to see it from so far off. It was probably also why it had been chosen in the first place.

Clint was riding Duke, his big, black gelding. He had left his rig and team behind this trip because he wanted to make better time. Not that he was in a hurry to get somewhere in particular. He just wanted to be able to move faster. More and more lately he just wanted to be on the move. You'd think that the older he got the more he'd want to stay in one place, but that was not the case.

He rode Duke up the hill, wondering what he intended to do when he got there. Would he cut the stranger down and take him to the nearest town? Or just bury him? Or leave him hanging?

All of these questions were echoing inside his head as he approached the hanging man—and then he stopped suddenly and stared.

It was not a hanging man, but a hanging woman.

Someone had lynched a woman!

He stared in disbelief. This close he could see that her shirt was torn in the front, exposing one breast. Her flesh looked stark white, and he found himself staring at her, feeling ashamed even as he did so. In life she had been a well-built woman. Her face was slumped forward, her hair hanging over it, and her hands had been tied behind her. Her legs had been left free, for kicking would only have made things worse for her.

Jesus, he'd never expected that it would be a woman. Now there was no question, he had to cut her down. He rode right up to her, took out a knife, reached above her head and cut the rope. As the body hit the ground he heard a sound like a grunt, but he assumed that the fall had driven air from her lungs.

He dismounted and went to examine the body. As he crouched over her, he couldn't believe his eyes.

She was breathing!

The hanged woman was still alive.

•   •   •

Carlos Lopez rode through the gates of the Triple-9 ranch and up to the house. He gave his horse over to one of the hands and went inside. He found his boss, Brian Wesley, sitting at his desk in his study. That had been where the man had been when Lopez first left that morning.

"Well?" Wesley asked, as his foreman entered the room.

"It is done, *Patron.*"

Wesley winced.

"Is she dead?"

"Yes."

"Did anyone see you?"

"No."

"So no one knows of our involvement?"

"No one, *Patron.*"

Wesley nodded.

"Good, good."

He did not say anything after that, so Lopez turned and left.

Brian Wesley swiveled his chair around and stared out his window. He rubbed his hands together, as if washing them. It was an ugly thing to do, he knew, but it had been the only way out for him.

The only way.

Denise Wesley watched as Carlos Lopez left the house. She was at the head of the stairs, and as the Mexican foreman closed the door behind him she came down. She stopped right at the bottom and looked down the hall toward her husband's office. She debated going back there, finally deciding that she had the right to.

As she entered, Wesley was still facing the window.

"Well?" she asked.

Without turning he said, "She's gone."

"For good?"

"Yes," he said, "for good."

"She better never come back here, Brian," Denise said. "If she does—"

"She won't, Denise," Wesley said. "I guarantee it."

Denise stood her ground for a moment, but when it became clear that her husband was not going to turn around, she turned and left the room, satisfied.

TWO

Clint leaned over the woman and removed the rope from her throat. She had a horrible rope burn that would probably leave a scar that would stay with her for the rest of her life—but at least she would have a rest of her life. He didn't know how she had managed it, but she'd been hanged and lived through it.

He got his canteen from his saddle and poured a little water on the woman's lips. She coughed, gagged a bit, then opened her mouth, and he gave her a little more.

She opened her mouth to speak, but nothing more than a rasp came out.

"You're all right," he told her. "I'm here to help you. Don't try to talk."

Her eyes fluttered open, and he was startled by their blueness. She stared at him and then opened her mouth to try to speak. Again, nothing came out.

"I'm here to help you," he told her again. "I cut you down. We'll camp here for the night. I'll make some coffee, and maybe by morning you'll be able to tell me what happened.''

She opened her mouth as if to speak, but he didn't give her the chance to try.

"Just rest," he said. "That's all you have to do for now. Just rest."

She closed her mouth and then her eyes. She was either asleep or passed out, but she was breathing regularly. Clint took the time to make a proper camp.

He made her as comfortable as he could while he built a fire and made some coffee. After that he rode around a bit and eventually found a horse, a chestnut gelding, not far away, still saddled and standing alone. He brought it back to camp and unsaddled it, putting the saddle behind her.

He used some water from the canteen to clean the burn on her neck. There was no need to bandage it because it had not bled, but it was as stark as the brand on a cow.

He watched her for most of the evening, and around midnight she opened her eyes and gasped, either out of surprise or from the pain in her throat.

"Hey, it's okay," he said soothingly. "You're all right."

She stared at him, her eyes very wide for a moment, and then she seemed to relax.

"My name is Clint Adams," he said. "Is that your horse you were on?"

She hesitated, then nodded. He had unsaddled her horse and gone through her things looking for a name.

All he'd found was a letter addressed to Esther Hayes.

"Are you Esther?"

She frowned, then nodded.

"I'm sorry, but I went through your things looking for your name. I didn't take anything."

She stared at him for a moment, then turned a bit to look at the saddle behind her. She touched it, then turned back and waved her hand in a gesture he took to mean that there wasn't anything to take.

"Do you want to try some coffee?"

She nodded and sat up, her back against her saddle—if it was her saddle and her horse. He poured a cup and brought it to her.

"Want me to hold it?" he asked.

She held her hands out and stared at them for a moment. They were steady, so she took the coffee from him.

"I don't know what happened to you, or what you did, but I can't condone hanging a woman. I don't know how you survived, but you did."

She sipped the coffee and closed her eyes tight as she tried to swallow. The second sip seemed to go down much easier.

"I don't know how long you were hanging there," Clint said. "Not long, I guess, if you didn't choke to death."

Gingerly, she touched the burn on her neck.

"From the burn the rope seems to have been stuck under your chin, leaving your windpipe free. Eventually, I guess, it would have slipped down and suffocated you."

She closed her eyes and shuddered. He had to admit, it was a pretty frightening thought.

She finished the coffee and held the empty cup out to him.

"More?"

She stared at him for a moment, then opened her mouth and said, "No." The word was barely audible, but he understood it.

"Hey, that's not bad," he said, taking the cup. "I don't suppose you'd like to try to eat anything?"

She shook her head. Obviously, the first "no" had taken too much out of her.

"Uh, you won't mind if I make some bacon for myself, will you?"

Again, she shook her head.

"I'm pretty hungry," he said, and tossed some bacon into a frying pan.

While the bacon cooked he kept talking to her, just making conversation, telling her where he had come from, but when he turned he saw that she had fallen asleep once again.

He ate his meager dinner of bacon and coffee, and hoped that come morning she'd be able to tell him what she had done that was so bad she had to be hanged.

THREE

Clint watched her for a while, until he started to get drowsy. He spread his blanket out on the opposite side of the fire and stretched out.

He woke up and looked up at the sky. He knew he'd been asleep but didn't know how long. He turned his head and saw Esther standing by him, looking down at him.

"Esther . . ." he said, but from the look on her face he didn't think she heard him.

He pushed himself up onto his elbows, and as he did she surprised him by quickly unbuttoning her torn shirt and removing it. The moon made her pale breasts seem to glow. Hurriedly, she removed her pants and underwear and then she was fully naked. Transfixed, he stared at her lovely body. She had a slender waist and curved hips, a deep belly button. The tangle of hair between her legs also seemed to glow in the light from the moon.

She abruptly pressed her hand down between her legs.

"Esther—"

She cut him off by dropping down to her knees and grabbing for his pants. She undid his belt and pulled his pants open.

"Hey—" he said, reaching out, but she slapped his hands away and glared at him angrily. It was then he decided she was probably not in her right mind at that moment. He didn't know what to do. Then her hand was inside his underwear, reaching for him, touching him, gripping him. She dragged his pants down over his hips to his thighs, then gripped his penis in both hands, bent over it, and took it in her mouth.

"Oh, jeez . . ." he said, dropping onto his back again.

Her mouth sucked on him avidly, her hands fondling his balls and holding his penis at the base while her head rode up and down on him. Suddenly, she released him from her mouth and mounted him. She held his penis and slid down onto it, taking him inside where she was warm and wet.

She began to ride him, frantically, grunting and groaning every time she came down on him. He lifted his butt from the ground, trying to meet her thrusts. He looked into her eyes; they were vacant. He didn't even think she knew who he was. She pressed her hands down on his belly, dug her nails into his flesh, increased her tempo, and then started saying something over and over and over . . .

He strained to hear what she was saying and finally thought he could make it out. She seemed to be saying the same two words over and over again.

"I'm alive ... I'm alive ... I'm alive ..."

FOUR

Clint woke the next morning before Esther Hayes. He made a fresh pot of coffee, the smell of which must have woken her up.

"Coffee?"

She looked at him, took a moment to place him and her situation, and then nodded.

"How about some water first?"

He handed her the canteen, and she took a long drink, wetting her lips and her parched, sore throat.

"Thanks," she said. The word was actually audible.

"You're welcome."

He took the canteen back and handed her a cup of coffee. She took a couple of sips and touched her throat with her hand. He studied her for a few moments, looking for some sign that she remembered what she had done—what they had done—last night.

After she had finished with him she had climbed off him, pulled her clothes back on, and lain back down to

12

go to sleep. He sat there for a few moments, then pulled his pants on and stood up. He walked over to her and leaned over her to satisfy himself that she was really asleep. He then went back to his own blanket where he sat for a while, shaking his head, before going back to sleep himself.

This morning he could only suppose that there was some part of her last night that needed to prove to herself that she was alive, and sex was the way she'd decided to do it.

"How do you feel?"

"Sore."

"I can understand that."

"And mad."

"That, too," he said. "Can you tell me what happened?"

"I got hanged." Her voice was deep, and he didn't think it was naturally so. It would probably take a while before it got back to normal.

"I know that," he said. "My questions are, why and by whom?"

"By mistake," she said. "By seven sons of bitches who appointed themselves judge and jury."

"Seven?"

She nodded, then looked down at herself. For the first time she noticed that her shirt was torn and one breast was bare. He noticed that there were bruises on her breast that resembled finger marks.

"Did they . . ." he started.

"No," she said. "One of them just decided he wanted a feel before they hanged me."

"I have an extra shirt," he said. "It might be big, but it will be better than that."

"Thanks, I'll take it."

He retrieved the shirt from his saddlebags and tossed it to her, then turned around so she could change into it. He felt odd doing so, since he had seen her naked last night, but apparently she didn't remember that.

"You're a gentleman."

"Thanks."

"Okay," she said, signaling that he could turn back around.

She had discarded the torn shirt and was drinking her coffee again.

"Do you know who the men were who lynched you?"

"Oh, yes."

"By name?"

"No," she said, "not by name, but I'll know them again when I see them."

"You'll be able to identify them to the law, then."

"The law?" she said, laughing then wincing. Her throat was not yet ready for her to laugh. "What would the law do?"

"Arrest them."

"On my word?" she asked. "Against theirs? Against seven of them what chance would I have in a court of law?"

He sat for a moment, thinking that over, and then had to admit to himself that she had a point. If she accused seven men of hanging her, they would simply alibi each other.

"I see you agree."

"I can certainly see your point, but—"

"But what?"

"What else can you do?"

"I can find them and kill them myself."

"Go after seven men alone?"

"I can take them," she said, "one at a time."

"Can you?"

She looked directly at him and said, "Yes, I can."

"Without a gun?"

She turned and looked at her saddle.

"That's all you have is a saddle. They took your saddlebags, your rifle, and whatever else you had."

"My pistol and gun belt."

"You wear a handgun?"

"Usually."

"Can you use it?"

"Yes."

Whether he agreed with what she was going to do or not, she was going to need a gun.

"Wait a minute."

He went to his saddlebags and pulled out a gun. It had recently been made for him by a friend, supposedly to replace the modified Colt which had served him so well for so long. He'd tried to use it, but eventually he'd gone back to his old gun.

He walked back to the fire and handed her the gun. She took it from him, and he watched with a critical eye how she handled it. It was obvious that she knew how to hold a gun; what remained was to find out if she knew how to fire it.

"This is a beautiful gun," she said.

"Yes."

"It's yours?"

"It was made for me by a good friend, but I can't give mine up yet," he said. "You can use it . . . until you get one of your own, that is."

"I don't know what to say," she said. "Thanks."

"I don't have an extra gun belt," he said. "You'll have to tuck it into your belt."

"I'll get a gun belt later," she said, setting the weapon aside. She looked past him and froze. He turned and saw what she was looking at.

It was the tree.

"Can we get away from here?" she asked. "Looking at that tree gives me the willies."

"Sure," he said. "We'll break camp and get going."

"How's my horse?" she asked.

"He's just fine."

"It was nice of them to leave him for me, huh?"

"I guess they didn't have much use for him themselves," he answered. "I'll saddle him for you."

"I'll do it."

"Can you?"

She stood and brushed her hands off on the seat of her britches, saying, "I think I can. If I need any help I'll let you know."

"Okay," he said. "I'll take care of the fire and saddle my horse."

He watched her as she saddled her mount, and although she struggled a bit she was finally able to get it done.

Clint stomped out the fire and saddled Duke, finishing just behind Esther.

"Are you sure you can ride?" he asked.

"I'm sure."

"What's the nearest town?" he asked.

"It's called Testament," she said. "About fifty miles west."

"I think Cromwell is that far to the east," he said. "Which way did you come?"

"I came from the north."

"Is that where . . . whatever happened, uh, happened?" he asked hesitantly.

"That's where I'll have to go to find the men who did it."

"So which way do you want to go now?"

"West," she said. "I'm smart enough to know I can't start after them now. I need to see a doctor, get some rest, and some clothes . . ."

"And talk to the law."

She didn't answer.

"Esther, you're going to have to at least talk to the law," he said. "You don't have to depend on them if you don't want to."

She shrugged and said, "All right. I'll talk to them."

She turned and took one last look at the tree he'd found her hanging from. The rest of the rope was still there, drifting in the breeze.

"Let's go," she said.

"Testament, it is," he said.

THE HANGING WOMAN   19

FIVE

Clint had been to a town called Testimony once, but never to this town called Testament. Actually, it wasn't much as towns went. It simply had enough of the right buildings—a saloon, a general store, and a jail—to be called a town.

Hopefully, it also had a doctor.

The livery stable was easy to find because it was the largest structure in town. It actually seemed too large and well made to be part of the town, but what Clint didn't know was that the town—such as it was—had been built up around the stable, which had been the barn on a ranch that had at one time stood there.

They rode to the stable and left their horses in the hands of the liveryman, a large, barrel-chested man in his forties with a wild, black beard. There seemed to be the remnants of several meals in it.

"Is there a doctor in this town?" Clint asked.

"Sure is," the man said. "Doc Cooper. Just go back

to the end of the street on the left and you'll see his office.''

''Thanks.''

Walking next to Esther, Clint could feel her exhaustion, but to her credit she had never once complained during the ride.

''After the doctor,'' he said, ''we can go and talk to the town sheriff.''

''Sure,'' she said, ''why not?''

She wasn't exactly dragging her heels, but she wasn't in a hurry either. She hadn't told Clint much about herself, or even why the lynch mob had decided to lynch her. From experience he knew that lynch mobs needed very little provocation, but there must have been something to attract their attention in the first place. Was she afraid that the sheriff would be attracted by the same thing?

When they reached the doctor's office he opened the door and let her go in first. It wasn't much of a doctor's office, which made it fit right in with the rest of the town.

The man seated at the rolltop desk must have been in his sixties. He put on a pair of glasses to look at them.

''Can I help you?''

''Are you Doc Cooper?'' Clint asked.

''I am.''

''My friend has an injury.''

''Oh? Where?''

Esther stepped forward and pulled aside the collar of the shirt she had borrowed from Clint.

''My God,'' the doctor said, ''that's nasty. That looks

like—well, it looks as if—uh—"

"It is," Clint said, "and she was."

"Hanged?"

"Yes."

"You poor thing," the doctor said. "Please, sit down. I have some salve I can put on it, but I'm afraid there's not much that can be done for the, uh, scar that will result—"

"I'm not worried about a scar," she said, "but my voice isn't usually this deep."

"Ah, well, there might be some damage to your throat. I'll take a look." He looked over her head at Clint. "I assume this was not a, uh, lawful hanging."

"No, it wasn't," Clint said. "A seven-man lynch mob hanged her."

"Cowards!" Cooper said. "Lynch mobs are cowardly, but to hang a woman . . ."

"I feel exactly the same way, Doctor."

"Well, I'll take care of your friend. If you'd care to wait outside . . ."

"Sure."

"You, uh, are going to talk to the sheriff when I'm done?"

"That's right," Clint said, "we are."

"Good, good," the doctor said. "Please remove your shirt, miss."

Clint went outside to wait.

SIX

"Well?" Clint asked as Esther came out of the doctor's office.

She stopped next to him, and he could smell the salve the doctor had put on her neck. It had a heavy, medicinal odor that made him wrinkle his nose.

"He looked down my throat and told me I was bruised and swollen inside. When the swelling goes down, my voice should return to normal."

"I kind of like it the way it is," he said. "It sounds . . . sexy."

"You think so?"

"Yes."

"Well," she said, "I don't feel sexy, especially not in your shirt. Do you think I could get something decent to wear before we see the sheriff?"

"Sure, why not?"

She hesitated a moment, looked down, shuffled her feet and said, "I don't have any money."

21

"I'll help out."

"It'll just be a loan."

"Fine," Clint said. "Let's go to the general store."

Clint thought Esther might want a dress or two, but she insisted all she needed was a couple of shirts and a new pair of britches. She kept insisting that this was a loan and she would pay him back.

Outside the general store she held on to the old pair of pants.

"They just need a cleaning," she said. "If there's a laundry in town—"

"You've put off talking to the sheriff long enough, Esther," he said. "We'll look for a laundry after that."

She hesitated and then said, "I'm hungry. The doctor said I could eat."

"If we don't go to the sheriff, Esther, the doctor will tell the sheriff that he treated a woman who'd been hanged. He'll come looking for us."

"I'll talk to him," she said, "but I want to eat first— and talk to you."

"Are you going to tell me what happened?"

"Yes," she said, "I'll tell you what happened."

"I met a man."

"Where?"

They were in a small café they found a block from the doctor's office. Clint decided that if there was such a place in Testament it would be better than taking her to the saloon.

She wasn't quite sure what to order, so she finally

settled on some homemade chicken soup that the waiter said they served. It wasn't very good, but it was hot and it felt good going down.

"A town called Horizon."

"In Kansas?"

She nodded.

"It's about three days north of where you found me."

"Was he married?"

She hesitated, then said, "Yes."

"And what happened?"

"He framed me for murder."

"What?"

She remained silent.

"Whose murder?"

"A man," she said. "A man I didn't even know."

"Why would he do that?"

"To get rid of me."

"Why?"

"Because he's not only married, he's rich," she said. "I guess he was afraid I was going to cause trouble if he . . . stopped seeing me."

"And would you have?"

"No. It was stupid of me to start up with him in the first place. Breaking it off was a good idea."

"So who were the men who hanged you?"

"A posse."

"With a lawman leading them?"

"No. There was no one with a badge among them."

"Was there anyone you recognized?"

"Just by sight. I saw two men who worked for . . . for the man who framed me."

"Are you sure he was behind it?"

"Yes . . . him or his wife."

"His wife knew about the two of you?"

"Yes, she found out."

"How could she have framed you, though?"

"I don't know. Maybe they both did it. Maybe they both wanted to get rid of me."

"When did all of this happen?"

"About a week ago."

"Were you arrested?"

"Yes."

"And?"

"I escaped."

"How?"

She laughed.

"Very easily."

"They let you escape?"

She nodded.

"I figured that out later," she said. "That night I just thought I was so clever."

"So the sheriff was in on it," Clint said. "He let you escape, but he didn't ride with the posse after you."

"But why didn't he?"

"Because he's the law," Clint explained, "and he couldn't go along with a lynching."

"Then he knew they were going to hang me."

"Sounds like it."

She put her spoon in her soup and pushed the bowl away, half finished.

"You believe me?"

"Why shouldn't I?"

"You don't know me."

He smiled.

"I know you better than I did when I cut you down, don't I?"

"I didn't kill the man," she said. "I didn't even know him."

"I believe you."

"But they arrested me," she went on. "How did they expect to prove I did it?"

"They didn't expect to prove it," he said. "They let you escape, remember? And then lynched you. As far as they're concerned, that closed the matter."

"Well," she said, touching her neck, "they were wrong about that. It's far from closed."

SEVEN

"Do you still think I should talk to the sheriff?" Esther asked. "There might be a wanted poster out on me."

"I don't think so," Clint said. "Not yet, anyway—and maybe not ever."

"Why not ever?"

"If you were framed they don't ever want you going to court," he said. "If some other lawman arrested you, that's what would happen."

"Oh."

"Besides, if they think you're dead why would they put out a poster?"

"They wouldn't, I guess."

"Unless they wanted to cover their tracks."

"What do you mean?"

"Well," he said, leaning forward, "maybe I'm putting too much thought into all of this, but what if they did a poster, knowing that you were dead and that no one would ever catch you?''

''But I'm not dead.''

''No, you're not.''

''Thanks to you.''

She leaned forward and touched his hand with hers.

''Have I said thank you yet?''

He thought back to last night, when she had practically raped him.

''No, not yet.''

''Well, thank you.''

''You're welcome.''

They both sat back in their chairs.

''So, are we going to see the sheriff?'' she asked.

He thought a moment and then said, ''No.''

''Then what?''

''We'll have to leave here before the doctor talks to the sheriff.''

''And then what?''

''Suppose you tell me, Esther,'' he suggested. ''What do you want to do?''

''I want to find them.''

''Who?''

''The men who actually lynched me,'' she said. ''I want the seven of them.''

He didn't ask if she wanted to bring them to justice or kill them. He thought he knew the answer to that.

''And then what?''

''What is there after that?''

''There's the person who sent them after you,'' he said. ''The person who framed you for a killing you didn't commit. That person caused the whole thing.

He—or she—needs to pay as well, don't you think?''

She hesitated, then said, ''I'd have to go back there.''

''Yes.''

''I can't,'' she said. ''I can't go back.''

''Yes, you can.''

''Not alone, I can't.''

Without hesitation he said, ''I'll go with you.''

''Will you help me find them, too? The men who lynched me?''

''I'll help you find them, Esther,'' he said, ''but I won't help you kill them.''

''You won't have to,'' she said, with a fiery look in her eyes. ''I'll do that myself.''

They left the café and headed directly for the livery. Clint would have preferred to stay a day, stock up, and then leave, but they couldn't do that now. There was no telling when the doctor would talk to the sheriff about them.

On the way they stopped quickly at the general store and picked up some coffee and beef jerky, just to keep them going until they reached the next town.

When they reached the livery and asked for their horses, the liveryman was surprised.

''Didn't stay very long, did ya?''

''No need,'' Clint said.

''Find the doc all right?''

''We found him.''

''Guess neither one of you is hurt so bad you can't ride, huh?''

"No," Clint said, "and we'd like to start riding as soon as possible."

The man took the hint and brought their horses out, saddled and ready to go. Clint paid him, and then mounted up.

"Where are we headed?" she asked as they left town.

"Do you know the town nearest to here?" he asked. "Between here and Horizon?"

She thought a moment, then said, "There's a place north of here where we might be able to get some supplies. From there we can start heading in a northeasterly direction for Horizon."

"What's this place called?"

"The last time I was there it was called Lullaby."

"Lullaby?"

She nodded.

He shrugged and said, "Okay, then let's head for Lullaby."

EIGHT

Clint was tempted to describe Lullaby as a sleepy little town, but he kept the description to himself.

It was about the size of Testament, but while Testament had seen its better days, Lullaby seemed to be on the rise. Many of the buildings had a new look to them. Even the air carried the smell of newly cut wood.

"Well," Esther said, "it's still called Lullaby, but it's grown."

"At least we'll be able to get what we need," Clint said, "and maybe a night's rest in a real bed."

"I could sure use that," she said.

They went directly to the livery, as they had done in Testament, and handed their horses over to a tall, rail-thin liveryman.

"Can you handle them?" Clint asked. He was more concerned with Duke than he was with Esther's chestnut gelding, which had no name.

"I been handling horses for a lot of years, mister," the man said.

"Sorry," Clint said.

He and Esther left the livery and headed for the hotel they had seen as they entered town.

"This wasn't here the last time I was through here," Esther said.

"When was that?" Clint asked.

"I don't know . . . three years ago, maybe."

"What do you do, Esther?" he asked. "You never told me."

"You never asked."

"I'm asking now."

"To tell you the truth, I don't do much."

"Which means that even though I asked you're not going to tell me."

She remained silent.

"Well, maybe when you know me better."

She looked at him then, smiled, and said, "Maybe."

They went to one of Lullaby's two hotels and checked in, getting a room for each of them. Clint still wondered about what had happened between them last night, whether or not she remembered.

Clint walked Esther to her room, opened the door, and handed her the key.

"Get some rest."

"What are you going to do?"

"I'm going to walk around, buy some supplies, maybe talk to the local law."

"About what?"

"Don't worry," he said, "I won't say a thing about you. I'm just going to make conversation and see what comes up."

"When will we be leaving here?"

"Tomorrow, bright and early. If you want you can sleep until then."

She smiled and said, "I'm going to want to eat."

"Solid food?"

"It's time to try, I think."

"Okay," he said, "I'll come back and get you in a few hours, and I'll buy you dinner."

"Why?"

"Because you're hungry—or you will be."

"No, I mean, why are you helping me? You didn't have to do anything after you cut me down . . . and you didn't even have to do that."

"Yes, I did."

"Well . . . you sure don't have to spend money on me, buy me clothes and food."

Clint smiled, patted her cheek, and said, "If I don't, who will?"

NINE

Clint found the sheriff's office with no trouble. There was a brand-new piece of wood nailed to the wall near the door with SHERIFF ALBERT UNGER written on it. He opened the door and went in.

The man behind the desk—a *brand-new* desk—was young, maybe thirty, and Clint wouldn't have been surprised to find out he was new to the job. For one thing he smiled when he saw Clint and said, "Hello, how can I help you?" like a store clerk.

Store-clerk-turned-sheriff, probably.

"Sheriff, my name's Clint Adams."

"What can I do for you, Mr. Adams?"

Not much, Clint thought. If the man didn't recognize his name, then he hadn't been in that office very long.

"I'm just passing through, Sheriff, and thought I'd check in with you."

The man frowned and asked, "Why?"

Very new. It didn't look as if Clint was going to get anything here.

"Just being sociable," he said.

"That's real nice of you, Mr. . . ."

"Adams."

"Right, right, Mr. Adams. How long will you be staying in town?"

"Not long."

"It's a growing town."

"I'll bet."

Clint turned and walked to the door, then turned back.

"Mind if I ask you a question?"

"Sure."

"How long have you been sheriff?"

"We had an election a few months ago," the man said proudly. "I won."

"What did you do before that?"

"I was the schoolteacher."

"Well," Clint said, "at least you had experience."

"Huh?" the man said, but Clint was out the door.

Clint walked around the town awhile, killing time to give Esther a few hours to rest. He wondered about her. She had told him next to nothing about herself, and probably wouldn't until she felt she could trust him. What more he had to do to gain her trust was beyond him, but he was willing to wait.

Why?

That was something he didn't even know. All he knew was that he wanted to help her. When he thought about her hanging from a tree, put there by seven men, a rage started to build up inside of him. He would have felt that way about *any* woman who had been lynched. The fact that he liked Esther just added fuel to the fire.

When his stomach started to growl he went back to the hotel.

When he knocked on the door to her room there was no answer. He knocked again, then reached for the doorknob and tried it. The door wasn't locked. He turned the knob and went inside. For just one moment he wondered what he would do if the room was empty, but it wasn't. She was lying in bed with the sheet pulled up to her neck. He stood still and listened to her deep, even breathing.

He walked over to the bed and stood there, looking down at her. She was fast asleep, and he almost hated to wake her. Suddenly, though, he saw her frown and heard her make a sound, and he knew she was dreaming. He also knew that it was probably a dream that she wanted to wake up from.

He reached down to touch her just as she gasped and started to choke. He shook her, but she wouldn't wake up. She continued to choke and gasp as he shook her harder. Finally, her eyes opened and by that time her face was covered with sweat. She stared at him, unseeing for a moment, and then she sat up and threw her arms around him.

"I was hanging again," she said. "I couldn't breathe, I was choking. . . ."

"You're all right now," he said, holding her tightly, "you're all right now."

He held her for a few more minutes and then laid her back down.

"You're awake now," he said. "Do you want to go and get something to eat?"

"Yeah, I do," she said. "I'm hungry."

"Okay, get dressed," he said. "I'll wait for you downstairs."

"I've got to wash up," she said, sitting up. "I'll be down in a little bit."

"Are you all right?"

"Yeah, sure," she said. "I'm fine."

"I'll see you downstairs."

Clint left the room and closed the door behind him. He was going to have to remember to tell her to lock her door that night when she went to bed. Then again, if her door had been locked was it possible that she could have suffocated in her sleep? Maybe he'd saved her life by being there to wake her up.

He'd have to ask a doctor sometime if it was possible for someone to choke to death on a dream.

TEN

It took twenty minutes for Esther to come down to the lobby. Her face looked freshly scrubbed, but there were shadows beneath her eyes. She was going to need a lot more sleep than she'd just had before those shadows would go away.

"How are you feeling?" Clint asked.

"I'm fine, really."

"It was a dream."

"I know," she said, touching her neck, "I know."

"Come on," he said, "let's get something to eat."

They found a restaurant called the Brickhouse a few blocks from the hotel. It was dinnertime, and it seemed as if most of the town was there, eating. They had to wait for a table fifteen minutes but finally got one by the window.

Clint wasn't comfortable sitting by the window, even though they'd only been in town a few hours and nobody knew he was there. At least the glass had the name of the restaurant stenciled into it, making it hard to see him from the outside.

"You want a steak?" Clint asked her.

"I think a steak would be too adventurous," she said. "I think I'll try some chicken."

"And potatoes," Clint said. "Potatoes are easy to chew."

"Okay, and some potatoes."

A middle-aged waitress came over, and Clint ordered chicken and potatoes for both of them, along with a pot of coffee.

"You could have had a steak," she said.

"I like chicken just fine."

The waitress brought the coffee and poured two cups.

"What did the sheriff say?"

He made a face.

"Up until a few months ago the sheriff of this town was the schoolteacher."

"What?"

"That's right," Clint said. "He's not going to do us much good."

"So what do we do?"

"We get a good night's sleep and get going in the morning."

"What about finding out about a poster?"

"Whether we know or not doesn't really matter," Clint said. "We still have to go back to Horizon."

"Horizon."

"That's where we'll find them."

"I hope so."

"I know so," he said. "The members of the posse

would have all come from that town. That's where we'll find them, all right.''

The waitress came with the food and set it before them. Clint watched as Esther picked up a piece of chicken, nibbled off a little, and swallowed.

''Bad?''

''Not too bad.''

She took a bigger piece, chewed and swallowed, and touched her throat.

''That was bad,'' she said, with a smile.

''Take smaller pieces.''

''I will.''

They proceeded to eat their dinner, Clint finishing well ahead of Esther, who did quite well to finish at all. She ate small pieces one at a time and eventually finished the whole meal.

Clint ordered a second pot of coffee, and they sat and drank it slowly.

Abruptly, Esther sat back and looked at him.

''I feel better.''

She looked better, too. Unfortunately her voice didn't sound any better. Clint wondered if the damage was permanent.

''You look stronger.''

''I think I could ride tonight.''

''Oh, I don't think so,'' Clint said. ''If you don't need the rest, I do, and so do the horses.''

''That big brute of yours?'' she said. ''He could go for days, and so could you.''

''We'll leave in the morning, Esther,'' Clint said. ''I could use a night in a real bed, remember?''

"Oh, all right."

"I know you're anxious to get to Horizon, but we'll find those men, don't worry."

"That's just it, Clint," she said, leaning forward. "I'm not anxious to get to Horizon."

"Why not?"

"I'm scared."

"That's natural."

"Is it?"

"Sure."

"What can I do about it?"

"You have two choices."

"What are they?"

"You can forget about it."

"What?"

"You're alive, they think you're dead, just keep riding. They'll never know."

"*I'll* know," she said.

"So what?"

"I can't," she said. "I can't just let them get away with it. Any of them!"

"Okay."

"What's my other choice?"

"You can go on being afraid, and do what has to be done."

"How can I do that if I'm afraid?"

"You're feeling two things, Esther," he said. "Fear and anger. Feed on the anger, and you'll be able to control the fear."

"It won't go away?"

"You better hope it never goes away."

"What about you?"

"What about me?"

"Do you ever feel afraid?"

"I'd be a fool not to."

"But . . . with your reputation . . ."

"I can still be killed, Esther," he said, "big reputation or not. But there's another kind of fear to be dealt with."

"What's that?"

"Have you ever killed anyone, Esther?"

"No," she admitted, "no, I haven't."

"There's the fear not of being killed but of killing."

"Why should you be afraid of that?"

"You've got to be afraid that it will get too easy," he said.

"And has it?" she asked. "Has it ever gotten easy for you?"

"No, it hasn't. It's never been easy for me."

She stared at him.

"What is it?" he asked.

"I just . . . you never know, do you?"

"About what?"

"Reputations," she said. "I mean, you're nothing like your reputation, so whose reputation could you believe?"

"I don't know," he said. "I can't speak for other people's reps, only mine."

She played with her fork for a few moments, then set it down.

"What do you think I should do, Clint?"

"I can't tell you what to do, Esther."

"What would you do?"

He hesitated a moment before answering.

"By telling you what I'd do I might be telling you what to do," he said finally. "Besides, what a man would do is different from what a woman would do."

"I don't think so," she said. "I think you'd go after the men who hanged you."

"I probably would."

"And that's what I have to do," she said. "I've got to make them know they made a mistake when they tried—when they *hanged* me."

"All right, then," he said, "we're back to square one."

"Huh?"

"We leave in the morning."

ELEVEN

Clint was relaxing in his hotel room later that night, just waiting for the night to pass so that they could continue on. He was thinking about Esther, and how much he trusted her. He really didn't know her. Could she have been lying? Could it be she actually *was* wanted in Horizon? And not just for a trumped-up murder charge but something real?

No, he didn't think so. He had to trust his judgment, and it was usually pretty good. He thought she was telling the truth. She was too convincing not to be, especially when she talked about getting even for being hanged. The fever in her eyes was not something that could be faked.

He walked to the window and looked down at the street. It was after midnight. If his window was open he knew he'd be able to hear the noise from the saloon down the street. He wondered if Esther was sleeping, or if she was awake thinking about tomorrow, and the next day, and the day they would arrive back in Horizon.

There was a soft knock on the door just then. He turned away from the window and took his gun from his holster, which was hanging on the bedpost.

"Who is it?"

"It's me," Esther Hayes said.

Clint opened the door. She was standing in the hall, shivering. Her eyes were wet, as were the ends of her hair.

"What's wrong?"

"I had a dream," she said. "Can I come in?"

"Sure, come on in."

She came in and sat down on the bed, folded her hands in her lap. She was wearing the extra shirt of his he'd given her that morning. It came down to mid-thigh.

He walked to his holster and replaced the gun, then sat down beside her.

"Can I stay here tonight?" she asked.

"Of course you can. Come on, we need to get some sleep."

He stood her up, walked her around to the side of the bed, and helped her get in.

"Are you coming?"

"I'm coming."

He walked around to the other side of the bed, stripped to his underwear, and got under the sheet next to her. Her body was hot, and when she pressed back against him he found that she was naked under the shirt.

"Clint?" she said, without turning around.

"Yeah?"

"Last night?"

"Yeah."

"I remember."

"You remember what?"

"Having sex." She pushed her bare butt back against him even tighter and said, "I remember."

"Yeah," he said, "I remember, too."

He moved his right hand between them to touch her butt, sliding his middle finger between her cheeks. She moaned and wiggled herself against him.

He slid his other hand underneath her, slid it inside the shirt. He touched one breast, feeling the nipple harden against his palm.

She turned over, and he undid the buttons of her shirt, peeled it off, and dropped it onto the floor. She slid her hands into his underwear, slid them down his legs, and dropped them on top of the shirt.

"Well," she said, looking up at him from between his legs, "while I'm down here . . ."

She used her mouth and tongue on him to tease him fully erect, then took him into her mouth. She was very good, and Clint had to reach down and push her away before she finished him too soon.

"Come up here," he said, pulling her on top of him.

She kissed him, pushing her tongue into his mouth. He slid his hands over her back and buttocks, enjoying the way her smooth, hot skin felt.

Abruptly, he clasped her to him and rolled over so that he was on top. He kissed her mouth, her neck, her breasts, lingering over each nipple, and then moved further down, over her belly until his mouth was nestled between her legs, his tongue probing, seeking, finding and savoring.

"Oh, Clint . . ." she moaned, reaching for his head. Instead of pushing him away, though, as he had done to her, she pulled him more tightly to her and urged him on. He used his mouth, his tongue, slid his hands beneath her to cup her buttocks and lift her off the bed.

"Yes," she whispered, "oh, yes, there . . . right there . . . oh, please . . ."

After that she couldn't speak, she could only moan and cry out, and then, finally, scream. . . .

"I'm surprised someone isn't breaking down the door," Clint said later.

"Why?" She snuggled into his arms.

"You screamed loud enough to wake the whole hotel."

She closed her eyes and said, "No one heard, Clint."

"I guess not." He pulled her close and said, "Go to sleep, Esther. There won't be any more nightmares tonight."

TWELVE

Clint opened his eyes just moments before someone started banging on the door. Esther was lying on his left shoulder. With his right hand he drew his gun from the holster just as the door slammed open.

The first man through the door had a gun in his hand. Clint didn't need to know anything more. He fired once, catching the man in the chest. The impact of the bullet drove the man back, knocking him into a second man right behind him.

The shot woke Esther, but she didn't have time to say a word. Clint knocked her off the bed and then rolled off the opposite side. He was down on one knee when the second man shoved the first man out of the way and entered the room himself, gun in hand. Clint fired again. As his bullet struck the man in the belly, the man discharged his own gun into the ceiling, then fell to the floor, doubled over, clutching his belly.

Clint rushed to the man, wanting to question him before he died. He kicked the man's gun away from him, then knelt next to him.

"Who sent you?"

"Oh, God, you killed me!" the man shouted.

"Who sent you?"

"I don't wanna die!" the man wailed.

"Well, you're going to die," Clint said brutally, "so you might as well tell me who sent you up here."

"Oh, Lord, get me a doctor. Mister, you gotta save me." The man clutched at Clint's arm, but Clint pulled away.

"Nobody can save you now, friend," Clint said. "You're gut-shot and you're going to die. Talk while you have the chance. Who sent you after me?"

But the man didn't answer. He whimpered and blubbered, and then blood bubbles appeared on his lips. Moments later, he was dead.

"Clint," Esther said. "What happened?"

He looked at her. She had gotten to her feet and was standing by the bed, naked. Even at that moment, with a dead man at his feet, he noticed how beautiful she was, how firm her breasts were, how smooth her skin was.

"You better get something on," he said, standing up. "We're bound to have company real soon."

She looked around for the shirt she'd been wearing when she came to him last night.

"You better take your own advice," she said.

"What?"

She pointed and said, "You're naked."

Clint heard footsteps in the hall and hurriedly grabbed for his pants.

THIRTEEN

Clint had barely gotten his pants on when the sheriff appeared in the doorway.

"My God!" he said. "What's been going on here?"

Clint couldn't help it. He imagined the man standing in front of a classroom full of naughty children, saying those exact same words.

"I think it's fairly obvious, Sheriff," Clint said. He found his shirt and put that on, too, shifting the gun from one hand to the other rather than putting it down.

"And what is this woman doing here?" the man asked.

"I slept here."

The sheriff looked aghast.

"Here? In the same room with him?"

"In the same bed."

"My God."

"Sheriff," Clint said, "in case you forgot, there are

49

two dead men on the floor. Who slept with who is hardly as important.''

''Yes, well . . . I'm just shocked . . . by everything. I mean, what man wouldn't be?''

Clint felt like saying an experienced lawman wouldn't be, but he didn't.

''How did this happen?''

''Look at the door,'' Clint said. ''They kicked it in and came in blasting.''

''I heard three shots.''

Clint was surprised that the man had heard all three shots.

''There's one in the ceiling,'' Clint said, and idly he thought how lucky somebody was that there was not a floor of rooms above them. He remembered a story about John Wesley Hardin killing a man in the next room by firing a shot through a wall. Having known Wes, he had always believed the story.

The sheriff looked up at the hole in the ceiling.

''Why did they do it?'' he asked.

''I don't know why,'' Clint said. ''I asked that one, but he was too worried about living to answer the question.''

''Do you know them?''

''No, Sheriff,'' Clint said, ''I don't know them.''

''Has this happened to you before?''

''Yes,'' Clint said wearily, ''many times.''

''Are you . . .'' the sheriff started, then stopped. He must have realized that by asking Clint who he was, he was betraying his ignorance.

As far as Clint was concerned it was too late to start worrying about that.

"My name is Clint Adams, Sheriff."

The sheriff looked at him blankly.

"Also known as the Gunsmith?" Esther said helpfully.

"Ah," the sheriff said, recognizing that name at least. Then he said, "Oh, so that's it."

"What is?"

"These two men recognized you and decided to try and make a name for themselves by killing you."

"That's one possibility," Clint said.

"Do you know of another?"

Clint looked at Esther. It had only just occurred to him that maybe the two men had been after her, but he decided not to voice that possibility.

"They could have been just robbers," Clint said.

"Why would they enter the room with their guns blazing?" the sheriff asked. Clint wanted to ask him if he had read the phrase "guns blazing" in some dime novel.

"I don't know, Sheriff."

"Well, I don't wonder that this happens to you, Mr. Adams. A man of your reputation."

It sounded as if the man was scolding him.

"I'm afraid I'm going to have to ask you to leave town."

"What?" Esther said. "Somebody tries to kill him, and you want to throw *him* out of town?"

"It wouldn't have happened if he wasn't here," the sheriff said, "and I don't want it to happen again." He turned to Clint and said, "I will ask you nicely once again to please leave town."

Clint was tempted to object, just to see what the man would do, but they didn't have time for that. They were planning to leave town today anyway.

"We'll leave just as soon as we get some breakfast and some supplies."

"But . . . the general store won't open for a couple of hours yet."

"Then I suggest you get them to open early," Clint said, "or we'll be here later than any of us want."

FOURTEEN

In spite of the sheriff's protests, Clint dragged the man on the floor out of the room and deposited him on the floor of the hallway, next to his friend.

"You can have someone else remove them the rest of the way," he told the sheriff, and closed the door.

"Clint," she said, "do you think—"

"I don't know what to think, Esther," he said. "Like I told the sheriff, this has happened to me before."

"But . . . they could have been after me."

"Why?" he asked. "Think about it. As far as anyone from Horizon is concerned, you're dead, probably still swinging from that tree."

She shuddered and hugged herself at his mention of the tree.

"It's more likely that the sheriff is right," he went on. "They recognized me and wanted to make a name for themselves."

"What if they recognized me?"

53

"Why would they," he asked, "unless they were part of the lynch mob?"

She didn't answer.

"You saw them. Did you recognize them?"

"I only saw the man in here," she said, "and I didn't know him."

"Chances are you wouldn't have known the other man either," he said.

He sat down on the bed to pull on his boots. Neither one of them would have time for a bath this morning.

"Let me get packed and then we'll go to your room so you can get dressed and packed."

"What a way to wake up," she said.

"Yeah."

"Especially after . . . well, especially after . . . well, you know."

He knew what she meant. They had awakened during the night and had made love again. This time there was no pretense on her part of being asleep or not remembering. She had participated fully.

"I know."

"Kind of ruins it, doesn't it?"

He stood up and took her by the shoulders.

"Only if we let it," he said, "and I, for one, don't intend to."

She smiled and said, "Well, I'll try not to let it either."

"Good," he said. "Now let's go to your room and get you ready to roll."

FIFTEEN

They went to Esther's room, and Clint looked out the window while she packed.

"What are you looking for?" she asked.

"I want to see if our two dead friends have any live ones," he said.

"You think there are more of them waiting for us out there?"

"There could be, yeah," he said, "but I don't think there are. The street looks pretty clear, except for the sheriff."

"He's out there?"

"Yeah, he's across the street, waiting to see if we leave."

"Clint?"

"Yeah?"

"What if he was in on it? What if he sent those men up here to get you . . . or me . . . or us?"

"I thought about that."

And he had. Suppose the sheriff *had* recognized him when he went into his office. Only what would the man's motive be? There was no reward out for him, and the sheriff wouldn't be able to take credit for the kill.

"But you don't think it was him?"

"There's nothing in it for him."

"What if he saw us ride in?" she asked. "What if he recognized me? What if there *is* a wanted poster out for me and—"

"Too many *what if*'s, Esther," he said, turning away from the window. "Besides, he's waiting out there alone. If he sent two men up to shoot us in our sleep, I don't think he'd be the kind of man to just wait out on the street for us this time."

"What if he's got—"

"I told you," he said, "there are too many *what if*'s."

"Maybe we should go out the back."

"We'll go out the front and over to the general store. I don't think we'll have much trouble from a sheriff who used to be a schoolteacher. Are you ready?"

"Yes, I'm ready." She didn't have much to pack, just what they had bought her in Testament.

"Then let's go."

When they walked out the front door, the sheriff crossed the street and approached them.

"You had breakfast already?"

"We decided to do you a favor and skip breakfast, Sheriff," Clint said. "Did you get that general store to open early?"

"I did, but Mr. Cummings isn't happy about it."

Clint assumed that Mr. Cummings owned the general store.

"That's okay," Clint said. "We'll be out of his hair—and yours—soon enough."

They walked over to the store together, and Clint gave the gruff owner a list of what he needed. The man supplied, and Clint paid the bill.

"Thanks for your help," he said to the man, who just growled and turned to the sheriff.

"Can I go have my breakfast now?"

"Go ahead, Stan. I'm sorry about this."

The three of them left the store together.

"You going to walk us over to the livery to make sure we leave?" Clint asked.

"I'm just doing my job, Mr. Adams. With you out of town there's less chance of any more shooting."

"You didn't happen to find out who sent those men after me, did you?" Clint asked as they walked.

"To tell you the truth, I haven't had time to ask around," Sheriff Unger said. "I'll do that once you're gone."

"Well," Clint said, "that makes me feel a whole lot better."

The three of them continued their walk to Lullaby's livery stable, and Clint noticed that the town was quiet at a time when it should have been coming to life.

Something was wrong.

"Sheriff?"

"Yes?"

"Is the town always this still in the morning?"

"Now that you mention it," Unger said, "no."

"You got many citizens that might be looking to make a name for themselves?"

"The men you killed weren't townsfolk," Unger said. "I can tell you that much."

"Strangers?"

"That's right, just passing through."

"Did they ride in alone?"

Unger hesitated, then said, "No, they rode in with two more men."

"And where are they?"

Another long pause, and then the man admitted, "I don't know."

They were within sight of the stable and Clint stopped walking. Unger stopped, too, with no objection.

"What's wrong?" Esther asked.

"Sheriff, any objection to the lady getting off the street?"

"None."

"Esther—"

"What is it?"

"Those men had two friends, and I don't think they're going to take the death of their partners very well."

"You think they're waiting in the livery?"

Clint nodded.

"Or somewhere between here and there."

"I've got a gun," she said, touching the butt of Clint's new pistol that was stuck in her belt.

"I think the sheriff and I can handle it, can't we, Sheriff?"

"I should go in alone—" the lawman started.

"You used to teach school, Sheriff, so I know you're

not stupid. Are you a foolish man?''

"What do you mean?''

"I mean if you try to do this alone they'll kill you. With me, you've got a chance.''

The sheriff studied Clint for a few moments, then licked his lips and wiped them with his hand.

"You better get off the street, miss,'' he said finally.

Grudgingly, Esther moved away from them and into a nearby doorway. She took with her the burlap bag that held their supplies.

"You're right about it being quiet,'' Unger said to Clint. "But if that means that people know there's going to be trouble, why didn't someone warn me?''

"You've got a lot to learn about being sheriff, Sheriff.''

SIXTEEN

In the last moments before the action, the sheriff made the proper decision and deferred to Clint's experience.

"My best guess is that they're inside the livery, waiting."

"Your best guess?" Unger asked. "With all your experience all you can do is guess?"

"It's an educated guess, Sheriff."

The sheriff remained silent but was not mollified by the remark.

"They'll be expecting me to come in the front to get the horses, so that's what I'll do."

"What do I do?"

"Is there a back door to the livery?"

"Yes."

"Then you go in the back."

"What if it's locked?"

"For my sake, I hope it isn't. If it is, find a window. Get inside any way you can."

This all sounded too haphazard to the former teacher turned sheriff, but he did not say so.

"We have one thing working in our favor."

"What's that?"

"They might not be expecting me this early."

"Why would they be expecting you to leave today at all?"

"After the shooting last night they'd figure I'd be leaving, either of my own accord or because you told me to."

"Why would they figure that?"

"It would be their best guess, Sheriff."

There was that word again. Unger guessed that if he was going to be a good sheriff he was going to have to start guessing more.

"All right, Sheriff, let's do it."

"Do what?"

Patiently, Clint said, "Work your way around to the back. I'll give you five minutes, and then I'll go in."

"Wouldn't it be better if we went in the front together—"

"No, it'll be better this way."

"How will I know when to come in?"

"Believe me, Sheriff," Clint said, "you'll know."

Unger wasn't all that sure.

"I still think it would be better—"

"Go ahead, Sheriff," Clint said, "your five minutes started ten seconds ago."

Hurriedly, the sheriff drew his gun and moved off. Clint wondered if any of this even mattered. If a man was watching the street from the livery he'd have already seen them walking toward the livery and then stopping. He'd already know that something was up, and that they were coming.

That would put the advantage squarely in his favor.

Well, Clint had the advantage against him many times before and had come out on top, and he would do so now. Besides, he couldn't afford to die now. He still had to help Esther.

Once five minutes were up, he started for the livery.

SEVENTEEN

From her doorway Esther Hayes saw Clint and the sheriff split up, and then minutes later Clint started walking toward the front of the livery. Was he going to go right in the front? She couldn't believe it.

She stepped from the doorway and started working her way further down the street. Clint had told her to stay clear of the action, but she hadn't agreed. She wanted to be close enough to help him, if he needed it.

She drew her gun.

Sheriff Albert Unger reached the back of the livery in three minutes and positioned himself at the door. He didn't try it to see if it was unlocked because he didn't want to alert anyone who was inside. There was a window right next to the door, though, so if the door was locked he'd go in that way.

He pressed his back against the wall of the livery, standing between the door and the window, and strained his ears to listen. When his signal to enter came, he intended to be ready.

Clint approached the front doors as nonchalantly as he could. He could only hope that someone wasn't taking a bead on him right at that moment from a window. He thought that they would probably wait for him to get inside. He'd be closer then and there would be less chance that they would miss.

The front doors were ajar. He wondered where the liveryman was, and hoped that he would not get in the way of the action. He also hoped that Esther would stay put, but he doubted she would. He didn't bother turning around to look, though. He didn't want anything to distract his attention as he reached for the doors to open them wider and walk into the livery.

But first he closed his eyes.

Inside the livery Bart Munch and Andy Beavis waited in semidarkness. Their eyes had already adjusted to the conditions in the livery. Clint Adams would be coming in from outside, and would not be able to see clearly for the first few seconds. That should give them enough time to gun him down.

They, along with their two partners—Lenny Andrews and Willy Lane, who were now dead—had recognized Clint Adams when he rode into town yesterday with the woman. It had been Lane's idea for them to kill Adams, thereby making reputations for themselves. He had decided that he and Andrews would bust into Adams's room while Munch and Beavis waited outside, just in case they missed. Well, they did miss and they got killed. Munch and Beavis had to disappear when the sheriff came running over.

It was Beavis who decided they should wait in the livery stable for Adams this morning. He figured the sheriff would either make Adams leave, or Adams would decide on his own. No point in staying in a town where people were shooting at you.

"Beavis?" Munch's voice called out.

"What?"

"How much longer?"

"Shut up."

"I'm gettin' a cramp."

"Shut up, Munch!"

"Don't tell me—"

"Shh, listen!"

They listened and both heard the front doors being opened.

Jesus, Beavis thought, don't jump the gun, Munch— but it was too late for that. As soon as the doors opened, letting the daylight in, Munch sprang from the stall he was hiding in, gun in hand.

EIGHTEEN

By closing his eyes for a few moments before opening the doors, Clint hoped that he'd be able to see better as he entered the livery. As it turned out it didn't matter. The light streaming in from behind him illuminated the inside, and he saw that man jump out from one of the stalls. He also saw the man's legs give out, probably from cramping. As he fell to the ground, though, he fired at Clint, who had no choice but to return fire.

At the sound of the first shot Sheriff Unger tried the back door. It was locked, so he ran over to the window and started knocking out the glass with the butt of his gun. Later he thought that he should have simply leapt through it, but at the moment that didn't seem a prudent course of action. After all, he might have gotten cut.

As Clint opened the front doors of the stable, Esther broke into a run, coming up behind him. She saw him shoot the first man, and then saw the second man come into view. She started to draw her gun, but before she could even get it out Clint had fired again, killing the second man.

Clint heard the glass breaking and heard footsteps behind him, but he kept his concentration, which was why he was able to easily dispatch the second man before he could fire a shot.

As Esther came up next to him with her gun in her hand he said, "I thought I told you to stay put."

"I didn't say I would," she said. "Where's the sheriff?"

They heard a grunt from the back of the stable, and the sound of a body hitting the ground. The sheriff then came into view, holding his gun in one hand, brushing himself off with the other.

"I had to, uh, use the window," he said sheepishly.

"A lot of help you were!" Esther scolded him. "Clint could have been killed."

"I told you, I had to use—"

"Never mind," Clint said.

He walked to the two men to make sure they were dead, then looked at Esther.

"You better get our supplies."

She nodded, tucked her gun back into her belt, and ran off to get the bag from the doorway she'd left it in.

"These men are all dead, there's no need for you to leave now," the sheriff said.

"Sheriff," Clint said, "I want to put this town behind me as soon as possible."

The sheriff looked hurt.

"It's not that bad."

"Take my advice," Clint said. "Get out of this business. Go back to teaching, and do it someplace else."

"Well . . . I'm sure I have a lot to learn—"

"You have *more* than a lot to learn, Sheriff, and I think you'll be dead before you get a chance to learn it."

"Is that a guess?" Unger asked.

"That's my educated opinion, Sheriff."

"Well—"

"You better look around for your liveryman," Clint said. "He's either tied up or dead someplace."

"Oh, my . . ."

As the sheriff searched, Clint saddled Duke. When Esther came in he helped her saddle her horse, and then he tied the burlap bag of supplies to his saddle.

"I found him!" the sheriff called. He appeared from the back of the livery and said, "He was knocked unconscious. I, uh, better fetch the doctor."

"Yes," Clint said, "you better do that. We'll be on our way, Sheriff."

"I, uh, I'm sorry . . ."

"You have nothing to apologize for, Sheriff," Clint said. "Just remember what I said."

"I, uh—I'll go and get the doc."

As the sheriff left the livery, Clint mounted up and called for Esther to do the same. To do so she had to move past one of the dead men, and she stopped in her tracks, staring down at him.

"Esther?"

There was no indication that she had heard him.

"Esther?"

Suddenly she started shaking. Clint dismounted quickly, but before he could reach her she had fallen to her knees next to the dead man and was beating on his chest with her fists.

"You son of a bitch," she was saying as Clint reached her. "You son of a bitch . . ."

"Esther," he said, grabbing her from behind, taking hold of her wrists and dragging her to her feet. "What's going on?"

"It's him."

"Who?"

"One of *them.*"

He caught on.

"One of the men who hanged you?"

"Yes, yes," she said, "one of them . . ."

Suddenly, she went limp in his arms. For a moment he thought she had passed out, but she had simply gone quiet. He released her and she remained standing.

"Can you look at the other one?"

She nodded and walked to the other body. Clint had to roll the man over for her to look at him.

"Yes," she said, a tear rolling down her cheek, "him, too."

"But not the other two?"

"I only saw one of them, remember?"

"All right," he said, "let's swing by the undertaker's so you can look at the last one. We should know whether two of them are dead or three."

"All right."

"Are you okay?"

"Yes."

"Come on," he said, putting his arm around her and walking her to her horse.

NINETEEN

Clint had to bang on the undertaker's door for a while before the man came down to open it. He insisted they couldn't come in, but Clint insisted that they had to because they were leaving town and they needed to take a look at the men he'd killed.

"You killed them?" asked the undertaker, a pale, pot-bellied man in his forties.

"That's right," Clint said, "and there are two more at the livery stable. Now can we come in?"

The man stepped aside nervously and allowed them to enter.

The bodies were in another room. Clint took Esther inside and said, "Take a good look at both of them."

They were both lying on their backs so she merely walked to them and studied them.

"No," she said, "neither one."

"Okay," he said, "let's go."

They left without thanking the undertaker.

• • •

As Clint and Esther rode out of Lullaby, he said, "Well, this is good news, isn't it?"

"Why?"

"Two of them are dead."

"But I didn't know that when you killed them," she said. "I want to *know* it's them when they die."

"And you want to kill them yourself?"

"Yes."

"Well, I'm sorry," he said, "but I didn't have the time to offer you the chance back there. Maybe next time."

She remained silent.

They rode a ways before she spoke again.

"What did you mean when you told the sheriff to remember what you said?"

"What?"

"The sheriff. What did you tell him?"

"To go back to teaching."

"Why?"

"He'd be a whole lot safer. Being a lawman is a whole lot harder than teaching school."

"Have you ever taught school?"

Clint looked over at her then, surprised by the question.

"Well . . . no," he said, laughing.

"Try it sometime," she said. "It's not an easy thing to do."

"Were you a teacher?"

"No," she said, looking straight ahead, "my mother was."

She closed up on him then, but he thought they'd made some progress. That was the single biggest piece of personal information he'd gotten out of her since they met.

TWENTY

The town they hit before Horizon was called Crawford. Clint had never heard of it, and as they rode in he saw that it was little more than a stopover. It had either stopped growing, or it hadn't started yet. His feeling was that it had stopped and would *never* start again. Still, it had what they needed: a general store, a saloon, and a hotel.

"Why don't we keep riding?" Esther asked. "It's only half a day."

"We need to talk," Clint said, "to plan. Also, I could use a hot meal. I'm tired of eating beef jerky."

"But we can get there by nightfall."

"We'd get there after nightfall, and I want to ride in rested, not exhausted."

"Why?"

"Because I don't know what's going to happen when I ride in with you. Do you?"

"Well . . . no."

"Then we need to make some plans for whatever might happen."

Esther finally agreed and they took their horses to Crawford's rather run-down livery stable. Esther shuddered as they entered the stable, remembering what had happened two days ago in Lullaby.

From the livery they walked to the hotel and secured a room from a bored but surprised desk clerk.

"Do I have an empty room?" he asked. "Take your pick. Don't hardly nobody stop in here anymore. To tell you the truth I ain't even sure what to charge you."

"Are the sheets on the beds clean?"

"I told you, ain't nobody been here, ain't nobody used the sheets. They're clean."

They went up to their room and opened the door. Esther wrinkled her nose.

"Musty," she said. "I'll open the window."

They had been sleeping together on the trail, so there didn't seem to be any reason to pay for two hotel rooms.

"Leave it open," Clint said. "It'll air out the room while we get something to eat."

They left the room and went downstairs, where they asked the clerk where they could get a meal.

"Saloon's about the only place."

"Thanks," Clint said.

They walked to the saloon and found it empty except for the bartender and one man sitting at a table with a drink he seemed more interested in staring at than drinking.

"New faces," the bartender said. "What'll you have?"

"Two beers, and a meal, if we can get one."

"I can make you some eggs."

"Any steak?"

"I doubt it," the man said. "Might have some ham."

"We'll take what you've got."

"How do you want the eggs?"

Clint looked at Esther and she said, "Scrambled."

"Comin' up," the man said.

They took their beers to a table in the back of the room, from where Clint could see the whole place.

"What are we going to do when we get to Horizon?" she asked.

"Well, we don't know if you're wanted for murder or not," he said, "since they think you're dead. Will people recognize you when we ride in?"

"I don't think so," she said. "I didn't exactly make a lot of friends while I was there. I didn't go out much."

"We can still tuck your hair under your hat and get you a bigger shirt, cover you up a little just in case. How many hotels in town?"

"Two."

"You stayed at one?"

"Yes."

"Then I'll get us a room at the other one."

"Then what?"

"Well, that's what we're here to talk about," Clint said. "Do you want to go to your, uh, ex-friend's ranch—"

"Wesley."

"What?"

"His name is Brian Wesley."

"I don't know the name."

"Well, most people in Horizon do, and in the county—maybe even in the state. He's got political ambitions."

"Then why—" Clint started, but stopped himself.

"Why what?"

"Never mind."

"You mean why would he risk that by seeing me? By making me his mistress."

"Well," Clint said, "it does seem chancy—"

"That's the way he likes to live his life," she said, "taking chances."

"A lot of people live their lives that way."

"Do you?"

"Most of the time," he said, "and it's not by choice."

"This is."

"What?"

"Helping me. You're taking a chance helping me. How do you know I'm not lying to you? How do you know I didn't deserve hanging?"

"I have to go with my instincts," he explained, "and my instincts tell me you're not lying—and even if you were, you didn't deserve to be hanged from a tree."

"No," she agreed, "I didn't."

"Then what do you want to do?"

"What are my options?"

"We can confront Wesley and ask him to give up the men who lynched you. We can send for a federal marshal—I don't know why I didn't think of this before—

and when he arrives tell him the story and put you in his hands.''

"How long would that take?''

"I don't know," he said. "It would depend on whether or not we could even get one sent here.''

"Too long," she said, shaking her head. "Clint, what do you suggest?''

"Okay," Clint said, "since you asked. We ride into town, get you into a hotel room, where you hole up for a while.''

"And what will you do?''

"I'll walk around town and see what I can find out. Maybe I'll hear something that will lead us to the men who lynched you. I can also talk to the sheriff. The mob that hung you was not deputized, and even if they were they shouldn't have been able to follow you as long and as far as they did, not without him.''

"And what about Wesley?''

"I can talk to him, too, and his wife. I can poke around a lot, Esther, and see what happens.''

"They might come after you.''

"They might.''

"You're willing to risk that for me?''

"Why not?" he said. "Like we just finished saying, everybody likes to take chances sometime or other. I guess this is one of my times.''

She thought about it for a few moments, then nodded her head and said, "All right, let's do it that way.''

He sat back in his chair as the bartender came with their eggs and said, "Let's do it.''

TWENTY-ONE

About ten miles outside of Horizon, to the north, Brian Wesley opened the front door of his house and stepped out.

"Where are you going, Brian?"

The voice came from behind him. It was the voice of his wife, Denise.

"I'm just going to town with Carlos, Denise," Wesley said.

Denise Wesley appeared at the door.

"You wouldn't have a new girlfriend in town, would you, Brian? Not after what happened with the last one?"

"Of course not, my dear," Wesley said. "I've already told you I learned my lesson."

"Oh, Brian," Denise said, "when it comes to women I don't think you'll ever learn your lesson. Sometimes I think the only way to keep you away from other women is to kill you."

Brian Wesley turned and put his arms loosely around

his wife. It was not the embrace of a lover. She had not felt his arms around her in *that* way for some time.

"You wouldn't do that, would you, Denise?"

"I don't know, Brian," she said, disengaging his hands and pushing them away. "Would I?"

She turned, went into the house, and closed the door behind her.

"Bitch!" Wesley said, but low enough so that only he heard it.

He went down the stairs and walked to the barn, where Carlos Lopez, his foreman, was waiting with two horses.

"I have news, *Patron.*"

"What news?"

"Of Munch and Beavis."

"Those two?" Wesley said in disgust. "Did they come back? Fire them."

"They have not come back," Lopez said. "They have been killed."

"Oh? Where?"

"In a town called Lullaby, about two days ride south of here. The sheriff there found something in their pockets that said they worked for you, so he sent a telegram to the sheriff of Horizon."

Lopez took the telegram out and handed it to his boss.

"Why should this interest me, Carlos?" Wesley asked, without reading it.

"They were two of the men who, uh—"

"What of it?" Wesley asked.

"They were killed by a man who was traveling with a woman."

"So?"

"The sheriff of Lullaby described her as having a scar, here," Lopez said, indicating his neck.

"What are you trying to tell me, Carlos? That the Hayes woman isn't dead? You told me she was dead. Hanged, you said."

"*Sí, Patron,* she was. I was there, I saw it."

"So?"

"Hanging a woman," Lopez said, shaking his head, "is very bad. Perhaps even a sin against God."

Wesley laughed.

"It wouldn't be your first sin against God, would it, Carlos?"

"But this . . . this was very bad. Her neck did not snap."

"What?"

"Her neck, it did not break."

"She strangled to death?"

Lopez did not answer.

"Carlos, are you telling me you didn't check to see if she was dead?"

"No, *Patron,*" Lopez said, "they left her hanging there and rode away. I also rode away."

"Jesus," Wesley said. "Well, she can't be alive. She would have strangled to death soon enough, right?"

"*Sí, Patron.*"

"Then what are you worried about? So these two jokers got themselves killed, so what?"

Wesley handed Lopez back the unread telegram.

"Come on, I want to get into town. I have an appointment with the mayor."

•   •   •

Denise Wesley watched from the window as her husband rode away from the ranch with Carlos Lopez. He didn't fool her one bit. If he didn't already have another girlfriend he soon would. The only thing she couldn't figure out was why he had chosen that Hayes woman, an outsider. At least when he took one of the sluts who worked at the saloon she knew her place. The Hayes woman actually thought she could get Brian away from her.

Well, she learned better, didn't she?

Denise had to be careful with the way she handled her husband. If he knew that she didn't care if he had a girlfriend he would probably stop cheating on her. No, it was thinking he was doing something wrong—like a little boy—that kept him doing it. And while he was sleeping around, he wasn't bothering her. Denise had learned long ago, at the hands of one of her stepfathers, that sex was not an enjoyable thing for her. Let Brian get it from someone else, as long as she got all of the other benefits of being Mrs. Brian Wesley.

TWENTY-TWO

Clint and Esther rode into Horizon late the next afternoon. Esther had her hair tucked up under her hat, and was wearing clothes that were too big for her. They went to the hotel first, where she stayed back while Clint got them two rooms. He got more than one room because they didn't want anyone to know that she was a woman. As far as anyone was concerned two strangers had ridden into town—two *men*.

When he got their keys they went up to one of the rooms. Once inside she took off the hat and shook her hair out.

"Do you think anyone noticed?" she asked.

"No," he said, "we had you pretty well hidden beneath those clothes."

"Speaking of which," she said, and began to unbutton the large shirt, which she was wearing over her own. "Now what?" she asked, tossing the shirt aside.

"You stay here. I'm going to take the horses over to

the livery stable. After that I'll take a turn around town.''

"And then we can get something to eat?''

"I don't think we'll be eating in public for a while,''
he said. "I'll bring something back for you.''

"Something hot,'' she called out to him as he was
going out the door.

As soon as Clint was gone Esther walked to the window and looked out. She had thought she would never
see Horizon again—first when she was leaving town,
and then when she was dangling at the end of a rope.

Somewhere in this town were the other men who had
hanged her, and they were going to suffer the same fate
as those two in Lullaby.

She hugged herself, feeling chilled, then walked to the
bed and sat down. She looked around the room and
hoped that she wouldn't be cooped up in it for very long.

Clint walked the horses to the livery, then took a walk
around town. Horizon was different from the other
towns they had been through recently. This one was on
the rise due in large part—according to what Esther had
been telling him—to Brian Wesley's presence and his
money.

He was impressed with the look and feel of the town.
It had vitality, a pulse that was almost palpable. It
showed even in the people, who walked briskly, as if
they all had a purpose.

As he walked past the sheriff's office he wondered if
he should stop in, then decided against it. First he just
wanted to hang around and see what he could hear on

his own. To that end he stopped at the largest saloon in town, the Purple Lady, and went inside. Dominating the wall above the long mahogany bar was a painting of a beautiful lady whose opulent curves were being shown off in a very low-cut purple gown—hence the name.

He walked to the bar, ordered a beer, and then drank it leisurely, taking in as much of the conversation around him as he could. This was often the best way to find out what was happening in a town.

For instance, just in the first ten minutes he heard the name Brian Wesley five times. It was obvious that the man was well-known, but also in listening carefully he discovered that well-known and well-liked were not the same thing.

The only men in the place who seemed to be speaking well of Wesley were the ones who worked for him. Most of the other townspeople had little to say, and what they did say was not good.

He spent an hour there and never heard any talk of a recent murder in town. He thought that was odd. A murder was something that did not soon go away.

He finished his beer and got out of the saloon before a fight broke out between the pro-Wesley and anti-Wesley factions.

He headed out in search of the office of the town newspaper.

TWENTY-THREE

Clint found the office of the *Horizon Beacon* and walked in. He was met by the clamor of the printing press. He wondered again, as he always did when he was in a newspaper office, how anyone could work around that noise.

The man running the machine saw him and turned it off. He approached Clint, wiping his hands on his apron.

"Can I help you?"

"I hope so. You see, I've only just arrived in town today and I'm very impressed by it."

The man smiled.

"We're real proud of it."

"I was wondering ... is your newspaper a good one?"

"Oh, yes," the man said, "it's excellent."

"I wonder ... would I be able to see some back issues?" he asked. "Just to see for myself?"

"I don't see why not," the man said. "I could bring you a couple of issues—"

"Could you bring me about two weeks' worth?"

"Two weeks . . . well, that's a lot—"

"I'd really like to try and get a feel for your paper," Clint said, "and I'd be learning about the town at the same time."

"Well . . . all right. Why don't you have a seat at that desk and I'll bring them out."

"Thanks very much."

Clint sat and the man soon appeared with an armful of newspapers. He set them down, told Clint to take his time, and went back to work.

Clint leafed through the papers very quickly, looking for any mention of a murder. He was surprised to find none. He was sure that any newspaper would cover a murder, if there had been one.

He stood up, waved to the man who had helped him— he never did find out if he was just a clerk or actually the editor—and left quickly.

On his way back to the hotel he stopped in a small café to pick up some food and brought it back with him in a wicker basket.

"It's about time," Esther said when she opened the door to his knock. She grabbed the basket from his hand, saying, "I'm starving."

There was no table in the room so she carried it to the bed.

"Did you eat?" she asked.

"No," he said, "that's for both of us."

She just about squealed with delight when she opened the basket and found the plump pieces of fried chicken.

Clint sat down on the bed so that the basket was between them and they started to eat.

"What did you find out?" she asked.

"That your friend—"

"Ex-friend!"

"That your ex-friend seems to be respected but not very well liked by the people of the town."

"I could have told you that."

"Then suppose you tell me why?"

"Because he thinks everyone should bow down to him because he's rich. He has almost no friends in town because he doesn't think that anyone is his equal."

"I've met men like him before. What about his wife?"

"What about her?"

"Did you ever meet her?"

Esther was raising a piece of chicken to her mouth and now she hesitated.

"Just once."

"Where?"

"In the jail."

"She came to see you?"

Esther nodded.

"Why?"

"She wanted me to know that I would never have Brian, that he would never leave her. She was very smug about my being in jail."

"Esther, tell me about the murder."

"Why?"

"Humor me."

"I was in the hotel room where we usually met, only instead of Brian the sheriff came and arrested me for murder. They wouldn't tell me who I was supposed to have killed, or how, or why. He took me to jail, I escaped, they followed me and lynched me. End of story . . . until you cut me down and saved it from being the end."

"Esther, there was no murder."

"What?"

"It's true."

"How do you know that?"

He explained how he had gone to the newspaper office and read back issues, finding no mention of a murder.

"If there was one, you know it would have been in the newspaper."

"Jesus."

"And one other thing. No one in town, or in the saloon, has even mentioned a murder in my earshot. If there had been one, people would still be talking about it."

"That son of a bitch!" she snapped. "Not only did he frame me, he framed me for a murder that never happened."

"You know what this means, don't you?" Clint asked.

"Yes . . . no . . . what does it mean?"

"It means there's no reason for you to hide in this hotel room," he said. "It means you can walk down the street without anyone pointing at you."

"And what happens when Brian sees us, or one of his men sees us?"

"Then he'll have to try something, won't he?"

She pointed at him with a chicken leg and said, "And we'll be ready, right?"

He smiled and said, "Right."

TWENTY-FOUR

When they were finished eating Clint said, "I think I'll go and see the sheriff."

"What for?"

"Just to ask some questions."

"About me?"

"I won't mention you," Clint said. "I'll just act like a stranger who's interested in settling down, and I'll ask him some questions about his town."

"Why can't I come?"

"Because that would be pushing it, Esther," he said. "The sheriff's bound to recognize you. You wait here and then I'll come back and take you out for a drink. How's that sound?"

She smiled and said, "That sounds just fine."

As Clint entered the sheriff's office, a man was coming from the back, where the cells were. He had black hair worn long and shaggy, and a mustache that had grown in spotty so that it did nothing to hide the fact that he had a very thick upper lip. He looked to be in his early forties and was wearing a badge that said SHER-IFF on it.

"Can I help you?" he asked.

"Are you the sheriff?"

"That's right, Sheriff Amos Kincaid."

"Sheriff, I just got into town and I'd like to ask you a few questions."

"About what?" The man's eyes narrowed suspiciously.

"Well, about your town."

"Why?"

"Because I'm impressed by it," he said, using the same story he'd used at the newspaper. "It looks like the kind of place a man could settle down."

"And that's what you want?" the sheriff asked. "To settle down here?"

"Well, I don't know if it will be here, but I am kind of tired of traveling around so much. What do you say?"

The man still studied him suspiciously, and it took a few moments for Clint to realize that this was the way the sheriff always looked.

"Whataya wanna know?" the man asked.

"Is it a quiet town?"

"It's quiet . . . because I keep it that way." Suddenly, the man's chest puffed up, and Clint knew he was the bragging type. This would work in his favor.

"Really? It must be a big job."

"It is, but I'm up to it."

He walked to his desk—or swaggered to it—and sat down.

"Do you have any help?"

"A couple of deputies, but they only do what I tell them."

"I guess that makes them good men."

"They're okay." Obviously, the man didn't want to say anything that would take away from his own luster.

"How about killings?"

"What?" That surprised him.

"You know, killings, murder."

"Uh, no . . . no . . . we don't have any of that here. I don't . . . uh . . . no, we don't."

"Really? That's odd."

"Why?"

"I thought I heard that there was a murder here a couple of weeks ago, maybe less."

"Where did you hear that?"

"Can't rightly say where I heard it," Clint said. "It's just something I picked up along the way."

"Well, you picked up wrong, mister."

"Maybe I can ask you—"

Looking somewhat deflated, the sheriff said, "Look, I got work to do. Find yourself someone else to ask questions. I ain't got no more time."

"Well, actually, I think you've already told me what I wanted to know, Sheriff. Thanks."

Clint turned and walked to the door, but before he reached it, it was opened and a man with the biggest jaw he'd ever seen walked in. He was tall, about thirty, and he should have been wearing a full beard to try to hide that jaw.

Their eyes met for a moment, and Clint knew instantly that the man knew who he was. He got out of there before the fellow could say anything.

"What the hell was he doin' here?" the man—who was called Jawbone—asked.

"Just askin' some questions."

"About what?"

"What's the difference? He was interested in maybe settlin' down here—"

"Not likely."

"Why not?"

"Don't you know who that was?"

"No," Kincaid said, "who was it?"

"Amos, that was Clint Adams."

"Naw," Kincaid said, his mouth remaining open.

"That's right."

"The Gunsmith?"

Jawbone nodded.

"Why the hell would Clint Adams wanna settle down here?"

"Men like him don't settle down anyplace, Amos," Jawbone said. "Now what was he askin' you? The boss is gonna wanna know."

Jawbone's boss was Brian Wesley, and at the mention of his name Kincaid began to sweat.

"Come on, Jawbone, Mr. Wesley don't have to know—"

"He has to know ever'thin', Amos, you know that,"
Jawbone said. "Now what was he askin' you about?"

Kincaid wet his lips and then said, "Murder, he was
askin' me about murder."

TWENTY-FIVE

Clint went back to the hotel to get Esther, who was now dressed in her own clothes.

"Ready for that drink?" he asked.

"More than ready."

As she started for the door, he saw the gun tucked into her belt.

"Esther, I think you better leave the gun here."

"Why?"

"We're going to attract enough attention going into the saloon together. If you have a gun we're really going to attract it."

"But isn't that what we want?" she asked. "Don't we want Brian to find out I'm here with you?"

"Yes, but—"

"And what if we see one of the men who lynched me? Or more than one?"

"Esther—"

"Clint, you're here to help me and I really appreciate

it,'' she said, ''but after being hanged once I don't intend for it to happen again. I want to keep the gun with me. I'll feel safer that way.''

He thought of several arguments to make, but never having been hanged himself he couldn't really know how she felt. If carrying the gun made her feel safer, then he thought she should.

''All right, then,'' Clint said, ''let's go.''

On the way to the saloon Clint told her of his talk with the sheriff.

''He was surprised when I asked him about murder,'' he finished.

''He should be,'' she said. ''If he arrested me for a murder that didn't happen, he'd wonder how you heard about it. He didn't know who you were?''

''He didn't act like it, and I can usually tell. Another man came in while I was leaving, though, and he recognized me right away.''

''Then he'd have told the sheriff by now, wouldn't he?'' she asked.

''I'm sure he has. He was an odd-looking fella.''

''In what way?''

''Well, he should have been wearing a beard.''

''Why?''

''He had the biggest jaw I've ever seen.''

They were just steps from the saloon, and she put her hand on his arm to stop him.

''Jawbone.''

''What?''

"That was Jawbone," she said. "He works for Brian."

"Was he with the lynch mob?"

"No," she said, "there was nobody from the Wesley ranch—the Triple-9—with the mob. I wonder where Jawbone knew you from?"

"It could be from anywhere," Clint said. "Come on, let's get that drink."

He took her arm and they walked into the Purple Lady. As expected, the entrance of a woman attracted attention. Clint spotted a table, walked Esther to it, and then went to the bar to get two beers.

"Do you know anyone here?" he asked as they sat.

"No," she said, "but then I didn't get out much."

"Well, do you recognize anyone from the lynching?" he asked.

She looked around, then turned back to him and said, "No."

They both took a healthy swig from their beers.

"They've all had a good look at you," he said. "If any of them recognizes you I guess we'll find out soon enough."

"Maybe we'll find out now," she said.

Clint knew what she meant, because he had seen the man enter even before she did. It was the man from the sheriff's office, Jawbone. Behind him the sheriff also entered, and he didn't look as all puffed up as he had in his office.

"They're coming over here," Esther said. "Jawbone will know me."

"That's okay," Clint said. "Just sit tight and don't say a word."

"But—"

"Quiet!"

The big man with the big jaw reached the table, and the sheriff stood just behind him to his right.

"Hello, Sheriff," Clint said. "Is this one of your deputies?"

"I ain't a deputy," Jawbone said.

"No?" Clint said. "Then what are you?"

"I'm a man who wanted to see what you were doing in Horizon, Adams, but now I see." He looked pointedly at Esther. "You're supposed to be . . ."

"Supposed to be what, Jawbone?" Clint asked.

Jawbone seemed to realize that he might have exceeded his boundaries.

"Dead?" Clint said, pushing. "Is that what you meant? You thought she was dead?"

"I just—"

"You work for Brian Wesley, don't you?" Clint asked.

Jawbone blinked and hesitated before answering.

"Uh, yeah, I do."

"Esther," he said, "show the man your neck."

It was her turn to hesitate this time, but she finally pulled her collar open to show the big man the rope burn scar on her neck.

Clint was watching Jawbone's face carefully and saw him flinch.

"See that? Tell your boss that his men botched the job. They hung her and she survived. Now she's back."

"Mr. Adams," Jawbone said, "I seen you in action and I know what you can do, but my advice to you is to ride out of town. My boss, he's got more men than you can handle working for him."

"Ranch hands," Clint said.

"Ranch hands, sure, but all kinds of men."

Clint looked Jawbone right in the eyes and said, "Men who hunt down a woman and hang her. I have no respect for, and no fear of, men like that. I also have no respect for your boss, Jawbone. You tell him that, from me, okay? Tell him Clint Adams has no respect for him."

"Mr. Adams," Jawbone said, "I'm gonna have to tell my boss just that, just what you said. Are you sure you want me to do that?"

"I'm more than sure, Jawbone," Clint said. "I insist on it."

Jawbone stared at Clint for a moment, and Clint thought that the man was studiously avoiding looking at Esther again.

"Come on, Amos," Jawbone said, reaching out and pushing the sheriff with one hand, "let's go."

"Well," Esther said, as Jawbone and Sheriff Kincaid left the saloon and everyone in the place was watching them, "now we're in it for real."

"Drink your beer, Esther," Clint said.

TWENTY-SIX

Jawbone and the sheriff split up outside the saloon, and the big man mounted his horse.

"You keep an eye on him, Amos," Jawbone said before he left.

"But—"

"Just watch him. You can do that, can't you?" Jawbone asked.

"I . . . guess so."

"You better do it," the big man said. Then he galloped off.

Back at the Triple-9 the first man Jawbone encountered was Carlos Lopez. Officially, Lopez was the foreman of the ranch, but in reality most of the men looked at Jawbone as being in charge. Lopez got paid for being foreman, but Jawbone didn't care about that. He only cared about working for Brian Wesley and doing the best he could for the man.

"You're late," Lopez said. "You were supposed to be back hours ago."

"I got a good reason," Jawbone said. He dismounted and handed his horse off to another man.

"What reason?"

"I got to talk to the boss."

"You talk to me first," Lopez said. "I am the foreman."

"Don't press me, Carlos," Jawbone said, squaring off with the Mexican. "I'll talk to the boss. You can come along and listen, if you want."

"I will do that," Lopez said, and they walked to the house together.

They were admitted to the house by Denise Wesley, who looked pretty as a picture in a spring dress that showed off her arms and a small portion of cleavage.

"What is it, Carlos?"

"Jawbone has something to tell the *patron, señora*."

Jawbone was looking down the front of her dress when she looked at him.

"What's it about, Jawbone?"

Jawbone colored at being caught, took off his hat and worried it in his hands.

"I think I better talk to him, ma'am."

Denise's face clouded. She stepped back and said, "Come in, then. He's in his office."

"Thank you, ma'am."

"*Señora,*" Lopez said.

The two men walked down the hall to the office. Lopez hurried to take the lead and Jawbone left it to him.

"*Patron?*" Lopez said as he went in the door. "Jawbone is back."

"Well, where the hell has he—where you been, boy?" Wesley demanded, standing up.

"I'm sorry I'm late, Boss, but I got somethin' to tell you."

"Like what?"

Jawbone turned around and closed the door.

"She's back."

Wesley frowned.

"Who's back?"

"You know . . . the woman."

"The . . . you mean . . . Esther?" Wesley whispered the name.

Jawbone nodded.

Wesley glared at Lopez.

"I thought she was dead," he hissed.

"*Patron,* I saw her hanged."

"She was hanged, all right," Jawbone said, "and she's got the scar around her neck to prove it."

"How?" Wesley demanded. "How did she survive?"

"I don't know," Jawbone said, "but there's more."

"What else could there be?" Wesley asked, sitting down behind his desk.

"She ain't alone," Jawbone said. "She's got a man with her."

"A man? What man?"

Jawbone took a deep breath and then said, "Clint Adams."

Lopez caught his breath sharply.

"The Gunsmith," Brian Wesley said.

"*Madre de Dios,*" Lopez said, and crossed himself. Wesley, an atheist, reacted explosively.

"Get out, goddamn it!" he shouted, standing up.

"But, *Patron*—"

"Get out of here, Lopez, before I kill you!"

To illustrate his point Wesley opened a desk drawer and took out a gun. Lopez quickly went to the door and ran out, leaving it open. Jawbone walked to the door, closed it, then turned to face his boss.

"Where the hell did she hook up with *him*?" Wesley asked, sitting back down.

"I don't know."

"You saw them together?"

"Yep."

Wesley put the gun down and said, "Tell me."

Jawbone told about running into Clint Adams in the sheriff's office, and then told his boss what Kincaid and Adams had been talking about.

"That fool," Wesley said. "What good is he as a sheriff if he can't recognize someone like the Gunsmith?"

Jawbone didn't have an answer for that.

"Did you talk to Adams?"

"Yeah, I did."

"You did?" Wesley was surprised. He hadn't expected the big man to say yes. "What did he say?"

"I think you should put the gun away before I tell you, Boss."

Wesley eyed the big man, then took the gun off the desk and put it back in the drawer.

"Okay," he said, "tell me."

TWENTY-SEVEN

Jawbone told his boss exactly what Clint Adams said, word for word.

"That son of a bitch," Wesley said. "He comes into my town and threatens me."

"I advised him to leave, Boss."

"He won't leave," Wesley said. "Do we have anyone on the payroll who can draw with him?"

"No," Jawbone said without hesitation.

"I thought you were pretty good with a gun once, Jawbone."

"Pretty good, yeah," the man said, "but not in his class."

"I'll have to find someone, then."

"Boss, you can beat him. You got enough men to go up against him."

"No," Wesley said, "that won't do. It won't look good for me to send twenty men to gun him down."

"Then what will you do?"

"Find someone," Wesley said. "I'll just have to find someone . . . but first I'll have to talk to them."

"*Them?*" Jawbone asked. "Both of them?"

"Of course, both of them," Wesley said. "They're together, aren't they?"

"But, Boss, what about . . . you know . . . Mrs. Wesley?"

"We'll just have to keep her from knowing anything, won't we?"

"How do we do that?" Jawbone asked. "She found out last time."

"Well, she won't this time," Wesley said.

"Whataya want me to do, Boss?"

"Sit down, Jawbone," Wesley said, "and I'll tell you. . . ."

Something was wrong. Denise Wesley knew it. She also knew that nobody was going to tell her what it was. She was going to have to find out for herself.

Carlos Lopez had left the house like a scalded cat, and her husband had been behind closed doors with that idiot Jawbone for hours.

She went upstairs to change into riding clothes. She wasn't going to find out anything by staying here. The answers were in Horizon, and that's where she was going.

When Brian Wesley and Jawbone came out of his office, Jawbone left the house and Wesley went looking for his wife. Unable to find her in the house, he went outside to look. At the barn he grabbed one of his men, who he thought was named Gates.

"Gates!"

"Uh, it's Cates, sir."

"Whatever," Wesley said. "Have you seen Mrs. Wesley?"

"About a half hour ago I did, yeah."

"Where?"

"In the barn," Cates said. "She saddled up her horse and then rode out."

"Rode out? Where was she going?"

"Can't say for sure, Boss," the man said, "but she looked like she was headin' for town."

"Damn it!" Wesley swore. How that bitch always seemed to know when he was trying to keep something from her was beyond him.

"I got work to do, Boss," Cates said.

"So go and do it!" Wesley snapped.

Cates scurried off.

Wesley went into the barn to saddle his own horse. He was going to have to figure something out, and he only had the amount of time it would take him to ride to town himself.

TWENTY-EIGHT

Clint decided that there was no point in parading Esther all over town. The sheriff had seen her, and Jawbone had seen her. Word was bound to get back to Brian Wesley. Walking her around out in the open would be taking unnecessary risks.

"I thought I wasn't going to have to be cooped up in a room," she said.

"I thought so, too," he said, "but plans change. Now that Wesley knows you're here, someone might take a shot at you."

"Or you," she said. "Are you going to stay inside, too?"

"No," Clint said, "but close to it."

"What does that mean?"

"I'm going to find a chair and take up position in front of the hotel."

"Just sitting?"

"Sitting and watching."

"For what?"

"That's what you're going to tell me," he said. "Describe to me both Brian Wesley and his wife . . . what's her name?"

"Denise."

"What do they look like?"

Esther started with Wesley, describing him as only a woman who had slept with a man could do. After that she gave him a brief description of the wife.

"Is she attractive?"

"I suppose."

"Would a man think so?"

Grudgingly, she said, "Yes."

"All right," he said. "Stay in and I'll see you later."

"What am I supposed to do?" she asked.

"Rest," he said, "think, make plans about what you're going to do with the rest of your life. Look out the window. If you see any of the men who lynched you walking down the street, come down and tell me."

"It would be easier if we walked around looking for them."

"It would also be easier to pick you off," Clint said. "Listen, if everything goes right we'll get their names from Wesley himself."

"Do you think so?"

"Like I said," he repeated, "if everything goes our way."

"Clint," she said as he walked to the door.

"Yeah?"

"Be careful, huh? You're going to be an easy target out there yourself."

He walked to her, took her in his arms, hugged her, gave her a kiss, and said, "I'm always careful."

TWENTY-NINE

Clint was sitting comfortably in front of the hotel when the woman rode into town. He knew immediately that she was Denise Wesley.

Esther's description of the woman had not done her justice. She had long, auburn hair that cascaded down her back, albeit a bit windblown at the moment. She reined her horse in across the street and dismounted. She was tall, most of her height seemingly in her legs, and she was full-breasted. As lovely as he thought Esther was, he wondered why a man married to a woman like this would have to cheat.

He watched her as she turned and surveyed the street. He had the feeling that she was looking for something without knowing what it was. Abruptly, she turned and walked down the street in the direction of the saloon and the sheriff's office.

He got out of his chair and followed her just long enough to see where she was going. As it turned out she went directly to the sheriff's office.

He went back to his chair and waited.

* * *

"I can't tell you nothin', Mrs. Wesley," Sheriff Kincaid said for the hundredth time.

"Can't, or won't, Sheriff?"

"It amounts to the same thing, ma'am."

"I don't know why all the men in this town are afraid of my husband," she said. Actually, it was a lie. She did know why they were afraid. It was because he had money and power.

"Mrs. Wesley, I suggest you go home—"

"I didn't come here for your suggestions, Sheriff," she said, cutting him off. "If you won't tell me what's going on, then there's no reason for me to be standing here talking to you. Good day."

She stormed out of the office, leaving Kincaid to mop his sweating brow with a dirty handkerchief. If he told her *anything* her husband didn't want her to know, Brian Wesley would have him skinned—or worse yet, take his badge.

* * *

Outside, in front of the sheriff's office, Denise Wesley surveyed the street. She looked up and down, and then her eyes fastened on the front of the hotel. If there were strangers in town stirring things up, that's where they'd be. Also, if her husband was keeping another woman she'd either be there, or at the other hotel. She decided to try there first.

● ● ●

Esther Hayes looked out her window and saw the woman walking down the street toward the hotel. She narrowed her eyes, trying to see better. She'd only met the woman once, but she felt sure that this was Denise Wesley.

She left the room and hurried downstairs.

Clint watched the tall woman walk toward the hotel with long, purposeful strides. The closer she got, the more of a fool he felt her husband was.

As she came closer he became aware that her eyes were less on the building itself and more on him.

She was curious.

As she got closer to the hotel Denise Wesley saw the man sitting out front. He was watching her, and she adjusted her walk. She knew men watched her and she enjoyed it and played to it. Most men, though, did not interest her in the slightest. She might even go so far as to say she hated men. This one, though, looked different. She didn't know what it was, there was just something about him that made him stand out. He looked like the kind of man women flocked to, and men steered clear of.

As she stepped up onto the boardwalk she was already forming in her mind what she was going to say to him. That all changed, however, when the woman came out of the hotel and stood next to the man.

It was her.

Esther Hayes.

''You little bitch!'' Denise Wesley said. ''You came back. How—''

''Your husband's men didn't get the job done, Denise,'' Esther said to Denise Wesley. She did not even notice herself that she had used the woman's first name.

''What are you talking about?''

Esther pulled her collar open and said, ''I'm talking about this. They strung me up to a tree, but I didn't die, and now I'm back.''

Denise Wesley gaped at Esther, staring at the rope scar around her neck.

''They . . . hanged you?''

''As if you didn't know.''

''I didn't . . . I didn't know,'' Denise said. ''My God, I wanted you gone, I knew Brian wanted you gone, but not . . . not dead.''

''No,'' Clint said, ''just framed for murder, and when that didn't work, hunted down and hanged.''

Denise moved her gaze from Esther's neck to Clint's face.

''And who are you?''

''My name is Clint Adams, Mrs. Wesley,'' he said. ''I'm a friend of Esther's.''

''You're together?''

''That's right,'' Esther said.

''You're here to help her get her revenge.''

''I prefer to think of it as justice, Mrs. Wesley,'' Clint said.

''Mister, let me tell you something. I'm shocked that my husband would have this woman . . . hanged, but that should tell you what kind of man he is. My advice to both of you is to mount up and ride out.''

"Can't do that, ma'am,'' Clint said, shaking his head. "We've got business not only with your husband, but the remainder of the lynch party.''

"The remainder . . .''

"That's right,'' Esther said. "Two of them are dead already.''

"You—you'd both better leave before my husband sees you.''

Esther looked past Denise Wesley and said, "I think it's a little too late for that.''

Two men had ridden into town together. One Clint recognized as Jawbone. That jaw was hard to miss.

The other, he rightly assumed, was Brian Wesley.

THIRTY

"Is that him?" Clint asked.

"That's him," Esther said.

Denise glared at Esther. None of the other women had been a danger to her, but she had felt from the beginning that this one could be. However, if her husband had had her hanged . . .

"Take my advice," she said, "both of you."

She turned and walked away in the direction of her husband.

"What was she doing here?" Esther asked.

"Your guess is as good as mine," Clint said. "You came out before she could say a word."

"I saw her from the window."

They watched as Denise Wesley walked over to where her husband and Jawbone were dismounting and tying off their horses.

"What's going to happen now?" Esther asked.

"My guess is he's going to want to talk."

"To you," she asked, "or to me?"

"That's the question."

When she reached her husband, Denise Wesley did not have a chance to say anything.

"Denise, what the hell are you doing here?"

"I knew something was going on, Brian, and I wanted to find out what it was."

"And now you know?"

"Jesus, Brian," Denise said, "you had her hanged?"

"I didn't have anybody hanged, Denise," Wesley said. "Whatever happened to her after she broke jail and left town I had nothing to do with."

"Well, you're going to have to tell that to her and her friend."

"Clint Adams."

"That's right," she said. "He told me his name—wait a minute." Her eyes widened. The name had not immediately struck a chord with her, but now it did. "He's not . . . the Gunsmith, is he?"

"That's who he is, Denise."

"But . . . how did she . . . what's he doing . . ."

"Denise," Wesley said, "go home. I'll take care of this."

"Brian," she said, "you can't go up against the Gunsmith."

"I don't intend to go up against him, Denise," he said, "I intend to talk to him."

"But what will you—"

"Go home, damn it! I'll talk to you about this later."

It wasn't often that Wesley raised his voice to Denise—not in earnest anyway.

"All right, Brian," she said. "I'll see you at home, then."

She crossed the street to her horse, mounted up, and rode out of town.

"Wow," Jawbone said, "I didn't think she'd go."

"Jawbone," Wesley said, "go over and ask Mr. Adams if he'll allow me to buy him a drink, and then bring him to the Purple Lady."

"Okay, Boss."

"And, Jawbone?"

"Yeah, Boss?"

"Make sure he knows I'm inviting him, all right?"

"Sure, Boss," Jawbone said, "inviting him."

"Right."

"The girl, too?"

"No, Jawbone," Wesley said, "not the girl. If I wanted you to invite the girl I would have told you to invite the girl. Just Adams, understand?"

"I understand."

"Then go on, do it."

As Jawbone started for the hotel Brian Wesley walked the other way, to the Purple Lady, of which he was—unbeknownst to most people in town—the owner.

THIRTY-ONE

"Adams."

"Mr. Jawbone."

"It's just Jawbone," the big man said.

"Okay, have it your way, Jawbone. Your boss send you over here with a message?"

"He sent me with an invitation."

"To what?"

"He wants to buy you a drink."

"Where?"

"At the Purple Lady."

"I've been there," Clint said. "Nice place."

"He owns it," Esther said.

"Really?" Clint said. "I didn't know that."

"Not a lot of people do," Jawbone said. "He told me I should make sure you know that he's just invitin' you."

"And me?" Esther asked.

Jawbone looked at her and shook his head.

"The invitation is just for Adams."

Clint looked up at Esther, and then back at Jawbone.

"You go back and tell your boss he'll have to talk to both of us."

"But—"

"Just tell him."

Jawbone looked as if he wanted to say more, but then he shrugged, turned, and walked away.

"Why did you tell him that?" she asked.

"I don't trust him," he said. "He might just want to occupy me, which would leave you alone here at the hotel."

"I have a gun."

"That reminds me."

"Of what?"

"We need to get you your own gun, and a holster."

"Why a holster?"

"If you're going to carry a gun it's better for you to have a holster, and not tuck it into your pants or your belt. It could get stuck just when you need it most, or go off when you need it the least."

She smiled then and said, "I think a man would have to worry about that more than a woman."

"I think you're right. Come on." He stood up.

"But . . . you just sent Jawbone to Brian with a message."

"That's okay," he said, taking her by the arm. "He'll find us. Let's find the local gun shop."

"I know just where it is."

He did, too, having located it earlier while walking,

but he did not say so. Instead he simply said, "Lead the way."

When Jawbone walked into the saloon Brian Wesley was sitting at a back table that was always held open for him.

"You're alone," he said, as Jawbone reached the table.

"Uh, yeah—"

"Why are you alone, Jawbone?" Wesley demanded. "Where is Adams?"

"He's still in front of the hotel."

"Why?"

"He says if you want to talk to him, you have to talk to the girl, too."

"What?"

"He said—"

"I heard you!"

Jawbone waited while his boss thought the situation over.

"He wants to be in control," Wesley finally said, "that's what it is."

"What do you want me to do, Boss?"

"We'll let him think he's in control for now," Wesley said. "You go and get both of them and bring them here. I'll say what I have to say to both of them."

"Okay," Jawbone said, "I'll go and get them."

"Yeah, you do that," Wesley said. As Jawbone was walking out, the man said to himself, "Just wait, Clint Adams. Your time is coming, real soon."

THIRTY-TWO

"What can I do for you folks this fine day?" the man behind the counter asked as they walked into the gunsmith shop.

"We need a gun."

"Certainly, sir," the man said, looking at Clint, "what do you have in mind?"

"Actually," Clint said, "it's for the lady."

"Ah," the man said, turning his attention to Esther, "what do you have in mind, ma'am?"

"Something that kills," she said.

The man seemed taken aback for a moment, but quickly recovered.

"I see."

"We need something light but with stopping power," Clint said.

"Well, let me see what we have."

He showed them several weapons, but they were all too big, or not big enough, or too old.

"Show me something you'd use yourself," Clint said, "or that you'd give to your sister."

"How about if I show you something I'm proud of?" the man asked.

"Let's see it."

He bent over behind his counter and came up with a cherry wood display box. When he opened it, Clint and Esther came closer to take a look.

"It looks like a New Line," Clint said. He had a little New Line that he sometimes used as a hide-out gun, but he hadn't taken it on this trip, or he might have given it to Esther.

"It's a variation," the gunsmith said, "called the New Pocket, from Colt. This is sort of a prototype. The gun won't even be ready for sale for several years yet, if not longer."

"Why do you have one?"

"Well," the man said hesitantly, "I didn't really get it from Colt. See? There's no Colt symbol or markings."

"Then . . . did you do this?"

The man smiled.

"I cannot tell a lie."

"For Colt?"

"No, I'm afraid I might have come up with something at the same time as Colt, only they have the money to mass produce, and test and test and test. I don't. I made this gun, and then found out about Colt's."

Clint looked at the gun again.

"Pick it up," the man said, and Clint did.

It was light and slender.

"Thirty-two?" Clint asked.

"The Colts will be thirty-two's, but I made mine thirty-six caliber. More stopping power. That's what you asked for, right?"

Clint examined the gun. It fired six shots, had a swing-out cylinder, and a four-inch barrel. Because it was so slender, though, it would be easily concealable. It would work in a holster, or as a concealed pocket weapon.

"Here, hold it," Clint said, passing the gun to Esther. She took the gun he had loaned her and handed it to him.

"That's a beautiful piece," the man said. "May I see it?"

"Sure," Clint said, unloading it and handing it over.

"A careful man," the man said, taking the gun.

He turned the gun over in his hands, examining it while Esther was getting the feel of the New Pocket. He stopped suddenly when he saw the initials on the grips.

"Do these initials—M.B.—mean what I think they mean?" the man asked.

"If you're thinking Mick Bolton, you're right."

The man's eyes widened.

"No wonder it's a beautiful piece. It's a Bolton gun."

Clint knew the reputation Mick Bolton had with people who knew guns.

"If you don't mind me asking," the man said, "why did Bolton make this gun for you?"

"We're friends."

"And why don't you wear it?"

Clint looked down at the gun in his holster and said, "It was supposed to replace this one, but I can't bring myself to retire this one yet."

The man was staring at the gun on Clint's hip, narrowing his eyes to see better.

"Is that a double-action weapon?"

"Yes," Clint said, "I modified it myself."

"Excuse me," the man said, "but are you Clint Adams?"

"That's right."

"Oh . . ." the man said, gaping. "You invented double-action before anybody did."

"Maybe," Clint said modestly.

"No maybe about it. If you could have patented it—"

"Same problem as you, friend," Clint said. "No money. I'm happy with what I've got, though."

"Jesus," the man said, "I'm so embarrassed now."

"Why?"

"I've been showing guns to the man who knows them best," he said, handing Clint back the Mick Bolton weapon. "I'm ashamed of what I tried to sell you before."

"Don't think anything of it," Clint said. "What do you think, Esther?"

"I like it," she said.

"Take it," the man said. "It's yours."

"You can't just give it away," Clint said.

"I can to you," he said. "It would be an honor for you to take this gun."

"But you made it—"

"Which means I can give it away if I want to," he said. He looked at Esther and said, "Please, accept the gun."

"Only if you let us buy a holster," Clint said.

"Deal."

The man came up with a holster he had made specially for that gun. They came up with a price, and Clint paid him.

"What's your name?" Clint asked.

"Carter," the man said, "Ambrose Carter."

"Thank you, Mr. Carter."

"Thank you," Carter said. "It was a pleasure meeting you, and doing business with you. My God, I didn't even know you were in town. I'd love to sit down with you and talk about guns."

"I don't know how much longer I'll be around," Clint said. "Why don't we just wait and see what happens?"

"That's fine, that's fine," Carter said. "It was just such a . . . a pleasure to have you in my shop. I got to meet Clint Adams, and see a specially made Mick Bolton. I haven't had a day like this since . . . well, ever."

Clint turned to see Esther strapping on the gun belt, and then sliding the gun home.

"Ready to go?" he asked her.

"I'm ready."

They said good-bye to Ambrose Carter again and went outside.

"This gun feels perfect for me," she said.

"Good."

"But I'll pay you back," she added. "This was just a loan, right?"

"Oh, sure," he said, "just a loan." He looked across

the street and saw a man walking, obviously looking for someone.

"Look, there's Jawbone trying to find us. Let's go and hear what he has to say."

THIRTY-THREE

They crossed the street and were almost upon him when Jawbone noticed them.

"Where did you go?"

"We were around," Clint said. "What did your boss have to say?"

"He says it's okay for her to come."

"That's real big of him," Clint said, "don't you think?"

"Yeah," Esther said, "real big."

"Hey," Jawbone said, looking at Esther, "you're wearin' a gun."

"That's right."

"But . . . you're a woman."

"It doesn't bother you that a woman gets hanged," Clint said, "but it does bother you to see a woman wearing a gun?"

"Hey," Jawbone said, "I didn't have nothin' to do with no hangin'."

128

"Relax, Jawbone," Clint said, "she already told me that you weren't there. You're in the clear."

"Let's go, then," Jawbone said.

"No," Clint said, "you lead the way. I want to keep you in front of me."

Jawbone stiffened.

"I wouldn't shoot you in the back, if that's what you're thinkin'," he said.

"You work for a man who has women hanged," Clint said. "I'm afraid I wouldn't put anything past you."

Jawbone stared at Clint for a few seconds, then started for the saloon as if he didn't care if they were following him or not.

"You're provoking him," Esther whispered.

"Just testing him, that's all," Clint said. "I have the feeling we don't have to worry about him all that much. He doesn't seem to be in favor of what they did to you."

They walked to the Purple Lady, Jawbone entering a good twenty feet ahead of them.

"Wait," Clint said, putting his hand on Esther's arm.

"Why? They'll be waiting inside."

"Let them wait."

She smiled at him and said, "I like this."

"What?"

"You're making Brian wait, you're in control," she said. "The one thing I never had when I was with him was control."

"Well, you've got it now," Clint said, and then added, "for the time being, anyway."

Jawbone appeared at the batwing doors of the saloon

and looked out, then turned and said something to someone.

"Okay," Clint said. "Let's go. We're probably getting poor Jawbone in trouble."

Brian Wesley watched as Clint Adams and Esther Hayes entered the saloon. He had to admit that Esther looked good. He remembered what had attracted him to her in the first place.

As Clint and Esther approached Wesley's table, Clint realized that they were once again the center of attention. Esther was a woman wearing a gun, and they were obviously going to be speaking with the town's richest citizen, Brian Wesley.

"Esther, how nice to see you again."

"Didn't think you ever would again, did you, Brian?" she asked.

"Actually, no, I didn't," Wesley said. "And you must be the famous Clint Adams."

"I'm Clint Adams."

The two men stared at each other for a few moments, and then Wesley looked back at Esther.

"Esther, honey, you're armed," he said. "Is that for me?"

"It's for my protection."

"And what do you think you need protection from?"

"From you and men like you," she said. "From men who would hang a woman."

"Hang," Wesley said thoughtfully. "You know, Jawbone said something about that, but I didn't know what he was talking about."

"He was talking about this," she said, and pulled her collar aside.

"That's a nasty scar," Wesley said. "I hope you don't think I had anything to do with it."

"There's one way you can prove you didn't," Clint said.

Wesley looked up at Clint, placed his hands in his lap, shrugged his shoulders once, and asked, "And how's that?"

"By telling us who was in that posse."

"And why do you think I would know who was in a posse?" Wesley asked. "You should be asking the sheriff about something like that."

"Oh, you know who was in it, all right, and Clint is being kind calling it a posse," Esther said. "It was a damn lynch mob."

Wesley looked shocked and said, "Well, if it was a lynch mob then I really had nothing to do with it."

"Why did you ask us over here?" Clint asked.

"I asked you over here to talk sense to you," Wesley said. "I didn't expect you to bring Esther. I suspect you didn't want to leave her alone at the hotel."

"You suspect right."

"Well, okay, now she's here and nothing can happen to her. Hell, half the town is here. Why don't you sit down, and she can sit at another table while we talk."

"I don't want her sitting in the saloon alone."

"Ah, you're a gentleman," Wesley said, "bravo. What if Jawbone there sits with her?"

Clint looked at Jawbone, who was standing off to one side with his arms folded. In his own way Jawbone seemed to be as much of a gentleman as Clint. Well, almost. At least, he had seemed horrified at the prospect of hanging a woman.

"All right," Clint said. He turned to Esther and asked, "Is that all right with you?"

"That's fine with me," she said, her eyes fixed on Wesley the whole time. "I don't want to sit at a table with him, anyway."

"Then we're agreed," Wesley said with a smile. "Jawbone?"

"Yeah, Boss?"

"Would you take Miss Hayes to a table and sit with her, please? Make sure nothing happens to her, all right?"

"Sure, Boss."

Clint turned and watched Jawbone and Esther walk away. There were no tables available, so Jawbone simply picked one and made the three men sitting there move just by standing and looking at them.

"He's very efficient." Wesley pointed to the chair opposite him and said, "Please?"

THIRTY-FOUR

Clint sat down.

"Beer?" Wesley asked.

"Sure, why not?"

Wesley waved his arm, and a saloon girl appeared with two mugs of beer.

"Thanks, darlin'," he said, patting the girl on her shapely butt.

"Your wife is a beautiful woman," Clint said.

The remark clearly caught Wesley off guard.

"Yes," he said slowly, "yes, she is. The question you're implying is why would I want another woman . . . like Esther?"

"Like anyone."

"I don't think we're here to discuss my . . . my reasons for being unfaithful to my wife, Mr. Adams."

"What are we here to discuss, Mr. Wesley?"

"How much?" Wesley said after a moment.

"How much for what?"

"To make you go away," Wesley said. "How much to make you go away and take Esther with you?"

"I don't think you have that much money."

Wesley sat back in his chair and stared at Clint.

"Really?"

"Yes, really. Does that surprise you?"

"It shocks the hell out of me."

"Because you think money can buy anything?"

"I've always thought that, yes," Wesley said. He admonished Clint by wagging his index finger at him. "You're shaking my faith in human nature."

"That's too bad," Clint said. "Of course, you could make the same offer to Esther. She might accept money."

At the mention of Esther, Wesley's hand inadvertently went to his throat.

"Do you think she might?"

Clint sat forward.

"If seven men had lynched you, could your justice be bought off by money?"

Wesley dropped his hand and said, "Probably."

Clint sat back.

"I believe you."

"Come on, Adams, look at history," Wesley said. "Anybody can be bought off for the right price."

"Almost anybody, Wesley."

"You're sure I can't buy you off?"

"I'm positive."

"Then what's it going to take?"

"Well," Clint said without hesitation, "for one thing that phony murder charge will have to be removed."

"Done."

Clint wasn't surprised by Wesley's agreement to that. It was the easy one.

"I'll also need the names of everyone who was in that lynch party."

"Ooh," Wesley said, playing with his beer mug, "that one isn't so easy."

"Why not?"

"Well . . . I've already said that I don't know anything about that."

"And you think that if you give me names it will mean otherwise?"

Wesley just shrugged in reply to that.

"Isn't there some way you could get the names without admitting that?"

Wesley stroked his cheek.

"And if I do this, you and she will leave?"

"Well . . . no, there's more."

"Like what?"

"Well, that would be between you and her."

Wesley stared at Clint, then frowned before an amused look came over his face.

"What are you saying . . . you're not proposing that she wants to call me out?"

"I don't know," Clint said. "She's convinced that you had her framed for murder, and then let her escape so that lynch party could hunt her down."

"Now, how would I get seven good men to lynch a woman, Mr. Adams?"

Now it was Clint's turn to look amused.

"Aren't you the same man who just told me that anything can be bought with money?''

"Yes, but hanging a woman . . ."

"That idea could only have been born in the mind of a sick man, Wesley," Clint said. "Don't you think?"

Wesley didn't answer immediately, and Clint decided to just remain silent and wait to see what the man would say.

"I've already told you," Wesley said tightly, "I had nothing to do with that."

"Who did, do you think?"

"I don't know," the man said. "As I already said, I could *try* to find out, but I'm not guaranteeing anything."

"Well," Clint said, "I guess that will have to do for now."

"Meet me back here tomorrow at this same time."

Clint sat back and drank some of his beer, even though being in Wesley's presence made him sick to his stomach. What kind of man comes up with a hanging as a way to do away with a mistress?

"Clear her of the phony murder charge and get us some names," Clint said, "and then we'll talk again."

THIRTY-FIVE

Clint stood up and walked away, leaving half of his beer behind. As he passed the table where Jawbone and Esther were sitting, he said to her, "Let's go."

"Don't I get to talk to him?" she asked, falling into step with him.

"Oh, now you want to talk to him?"

"I only—"

"Wait until we get outside."

Once they were on the street she turned to him and asked, "What happened?"

He told her what they had talked about and what they'd agreed to.

"So he refuses to admit that he sent that lynch mob after me?"

"Yes."

"But not that he framed me for murder?"

"Right."

"That's not good enough."

She turned to go back in, and he grabbed her arm to stop her.

"Just hold on a minute," he said. "You didn't let me finish."

"What?"

"He's going to have the phony murder charge fixed."

"That's big of him."

"And he said he'll try to get us some names of the lynch mob posse."

"And he's going to do that without admitting that he was behind it?"

"Yes."

"How many names do you think he'll give us?"

"If he gives us one legitimate name we'll be able to get the rest from that person."

"And you think he'll give that to us?"

"I think he's the kind of man who would throw somebody to the wolves if it would help him, don't you?"

"You have to ask?"

"So do you still want to go in and talk to him?"

"No," she said, "not now. Not until we see what he gives us."

"Okay, then," he said. "We might as well go and get some dinner."

"I'm not hungry."

"Then I'll eat and you watch," Clint said. "One of us has to keep their strength up."

Jawbone stayed where he was until Wesley crooked his finger at him. The big man stood up, walked to the table, and sat in the chair vacated by Clint Adams.

"Whataya want me to do, Boss?"

"Find Ollie Grant—"

"What for?"

"Shut up until I'm done!"

"Yessir."

"Find Grant, pay him off, and tell him to get out of town."

"But why?"

"There's no reason I should be telling you this, Jawbone," Wesley said, "but I am. I don't want a word of this to get out, though. Understand?"

"You can count on me, Boss."

Wesley knew that was true. Jawbone was not the smartest man he had working for him, but he was the most loyal.

"Okay," he said, "I just made a deal with Adams and it includes Ollie Grant."

"So you're warning Grant to get out of town so Adams won't be able to find him, even if you give him up."

"Right." Maybe the big man wasn't so dumb after all.

"I get it."

"Then do it."

"I'll need some money."

"Right," Wesley said. "Come into the office with me."

They both stood up and went to a door in the back wall. It led to Wesley's office. While Jawbone waited, Wesley went to a hidden safe, opened it, and counted

out a certain amount of money that he thought would
make being on the run worth it to a man like Ollie Grant.
Grant, he knew, was part of the lynch posse, but he was
ordinarily just a layabout who was not valuable to either
him or to the town. Horizon could certainly get along
without the services of Ollie Grant.

"Here," Wesley said. He knew he didn't have to
warn Jawbone to make sure that Grant got every penny.

Jawbone tucked the money away in a pocket.

"What about the others?"

With the two Adams had already killed, and sending
Ollie Grant on the run, there were four other members
of the posse.

"I should give them all up after what they did," Wesley said.

"You mean you didn't tell them to lynch her?"

"I told them to chase her as far away from here as
they could," Wesley said. "I told them I didn't want
her coming back here. I told them to scare the hell out
of her. I guess things kind of went too far."

"I guess so."

Jawbone was relieved that the lynching had not been
Brian Wesley's idea. It never occurred to him that his
boss might be lying to him.

"Okay, now you know what to do with Grant, right?"
Wesley asked.

"Yes, Boss."

"Okay, when you've done that, find Ted Shelton."

"Shelton?" Jawbone asked. "He was part of that
lynch party, too, wasn't he?"

"That's right, he was."

"Why do you want him?"

"Just get to it, Jawbone," Wesley said, sitting behind his desk. "Find Ollie and get him gone, and find Shelton and get him here. No more questions."

"Yes, sir."

THIRTY-SIX

After dinner Clint and Esther went back to the hotel.

"I think we should stay in one room tonight," Clint said as they walked down the hall.

"Oh? What do you have in mind?"

They stopped in front of her door, and he put his arms around her waist.

"That, too," he said, "but also so we can look after one another."

"You think Brian would send someone after us during the night?"

"I think anything's possible," Clint said. Then he added to himself, especially when you're dealing with a man who would have a woman hanged.

"Well, all right, then," she said, opening her door and drawing him inside. "Is my room okay?"

He closed the door behind them and said, "Your room will do just fine."

• • •

Clint found Esther to be a voracious lover. She seemed to have an appetite that was never satisfied, and he wondered if she had been that way before the hanging. Maybe she realized that she needed to enjoy every moment of her life, because you never knew when it would end.

They undressed each other and fell onto the bed together. She twisted and squirmed as he tried to keep her beneath him, and finally he allowed her to get on top of him. She sat on him, pinning his penis between them, took his face in her hands and kissed him deeply. He reached to cup her breasts, brushing the nipples with his thumbs, making them harden.

She moved a bit to free his penis, then rubbed herself against it, wetting it. She closed her eyes as she continued to rub up against him, using his hardness to seek her pleasure without actually taking him inside, yet. She couldn't stand much of that, however, and finally lifted her hips. He poked inside of her easily, as she was slick and wet, and she began to ride him. From the times that they had made love, he had come to realize that she liked this position very much. Again he wondered if she had only enjoyed this dominant position since the hanging. It gave the illusion that she was in charge, even though he knew he could flip her over onto her back anytime he wanted to. He didn't want to do that, though . . . not yet, anyway.

THIRTY-SEVEN

When Jawbone returned to the saloon, he had Ted Shelton with him.

"Did you get to Grant?" Wesley asked.

"I did, Boss."

"And?"

"He didn't want to go, but I gave him the money and convinced him he should."

"Good."

"What's this all about?" Shelton asked. "I was headin' for the cathouse to scratch an itch when your big goon said you wanted to see me."

"Sit down, Ted," Wesley said. "This'll scratch another kind of itch for you."

Shelton sat and Jawbone started to sit.

"Not you, Jawbone," Wesley said. "I want to talk to Shelton alone."

Jawbone stopped, straightened up, and walked away without a word, but with a hurt look on his face.

"What's goin' on?" Shelton asked.

Wesley leaned forward and lowered his voice. It was late, and the saloon was getting ready to close, so it wasn't very noisy. He didn't want his voice to carry.

"Do you remember that matter I had you take care of for me?" he asked.

"If it's the one I think it is, yeah. So?"

"Well, it didn't—" Wesley stopped, realizing that he was raising his voice. He continued, keeping his voice lower but allowing some urgency to creep into it. "Well, you botched it up."

"Whataya mean?" Shelton asked. "We stretched her neck—"

"Shut up!" Wesley hissed. "She's alive, and she's here in town."

Shelton looked shocked.

"That can't be," he said, keeping his own voice down now. "I saw her swingin'."

"Well, I talked to her a few hours ago, right here— and she's got a man with her."

"What did they want?"

"They're looking for you."

"Me?"

"You and the rest of them."

"How do they know who we are?"

"They killed Munch and Beavis," Wesley said. "They must have gotten the names from them."

"Where are they?"

"They have rooms at the Stratton Hotel," Wesley said.

Shelton frowned as something occurred to him.

"Why did you have Jawbone warn Grant out of town?" he asked.

"Because Grant would talk if they got to him," Wesley said. "The rest of you won't. Can you get to the others?"

"Sure, but—"

"You better do something quick," Wesley said. "I don't want the girl and the man she's with getting you, too."

Shelton squared his jaw.

"They ain't gonna get us," he said. "I'll get the others and we'll take care of this tonight."

"Better you do it in the morning," Wesley said. "The girl is still wanted for murder. Nobody would blame you."

"That's a good idea," Shelton said. He stood up. "I don't know how she survived the hanging, Mr. Wesley, but she ain't gonna survive another day."

"That's good news, Ted," Wesley said, sitting back, "that's very good news."

Wesley watched as the bartender let Ted Shelton out the front door. Jawbone was still standing at the bar, nursing a beer and his hurt feelings.

Wesley got up, walked to the bar, and clapped Jawbone soundly on the shoulder.

"Come on, big fella," he said, "it's time to go home."

He didn't want to be around Horizon in the morning, when the fireworks started.

THIRTY-EIGHT

They fell into an exhausted sleep after making love for a very long time. Soon, she was awakening him by nuzzling his penis with her nose. He opened his eyes as she touched him with her tongue, licking him until he was hard, and then taking him into her mouth. She sucked on him as if her life depended on it, and when he exploded she kept him in her mouth until he was drained.

"I'm sorry," she said, snuggling up to him again, holding his limp, satisfied penis in one hand.

"For what?" he asked.

"For waking you. I woke up and I just wanted you so bad."

"That's all right," he said. "You can wake me up that way anytime."

"Clint?"

"Hmm?"

"What's going to happen after we're finished here?"

"I don't know," he said. "I'm not sure what you're asking."

She hesitated, then said, "I think you are."

"I think we'll go our separate ways, Esther," he said gently. "Is that a problem?"

"I hope it won't be," she said. "You know . . . I'm scared a lot of the time."

"I know."

"It's only being with you that's keeping me together."

"That will change."

"Will it?"

"Sure," he said. "Eventually you'll get back to living your life, like you did before."

"I wasn't really living before," she said. "I was just . . . existing. I was traveling, looking for . . . I don't even know what I was looking for."

"And you found yourself here, with Brian Wesley."

"Yes."

They were quiet for a few seconds, as if she was waiting for him to say something, maybe take her to task for getting involved with a married man.

"Have you ever been with a married woman?" she asked, surprising him.

"Yes, I have."

"But you're not proud of it, are you?"

"No."

"Well, I'm not proud of what I did, either. I never expected him to leave his wife for me, you know? I don't know why he felt he had to get rid of me the way he did, rather than just telling me it was over."

"I don't know, Esther," he said, holding her close. "Maybe that's something we can find out before we finally leave here."

"I hope so," she said sleepily.

Clint was awakened in the morning by a beam of light that came streaming through the window. Esther was lying next to him but not on his arm, so he was able to slip from the bed without waking her. His intention was to draw the curtain across the window to block out that sunlight, but as he reached the window he looked out and saw four men across the street. He backed away from the window quickly, so that he could still see them but they couldn't see him. They were all armed and watching the front of the hotel. They were standing roughly ten feet apart, and Clint instinctively knew that they were there for him and Esther.

He turned and went back to the bed, walking lightly as if he thought the men on the street might realize he was awake.

"Esther," he said, shaking her awake. "Esther."

"Hmm?"

"Come on, wake up."

"What is it?" She opened her eyes and stared at him. "What's wrong?"

"Wipe the sleep from your eyes," he said. "There's something I want you to see."

THIRTY-NINE

"Yes."

"All of them?" Clint asked.

"I can't tell," she said, "but I see two of them."

"This is Wesley's work."

They both moved away from the window.

"You think Brian sent them to kill us?"

"Sure," Clint said, "how else would they know where we were?"

"But . . . how can they justify just shooting us down when we leave the hotel?"

"He probably didn't do anything about that phony murder charge against you," Clint said. "In this town, it'll stand up when those yahoos gun us down."

"Then what do we do?"

"We'll have to go out the back door—if there is one," he said.

"And run?"

"No," he said, "and surprise them."

"Just the two of us against the four of them?" she asked.

"No," Clint said, "just me against the four of them."

"Do you think you can handle them?" she asked. "All four?"

"I'll have the element of surprise on my side."

"And me."

"Esther, I told you—"

"Why did you buy me this gun if you're not going to let me help?" she asked. "Was it just to humor me and keep me quiet?"

"That's not it—"

"You know I can shoot."

They had done some target shooting on the trail and it was true, she had been able to hit what she aimed at.

"At targets, yes, but you've never fired at a man and, more importantly, you've never fired at a man who was shooting back."

"Everybody's got to try sometime." She started to get dressed.

"Esther—"

"Clint, if you don't let me help, so help me, I'll walk out the front door."

"You'd be killed on the spot."

"I'm already supposed to be dead," she said. "I'm living on borrowed time anyway."

He stared at her, trying to decide whether or not she was serious. He finally decided she was.

"All right," he said. "Get dressed, strap on your gun, and listen to what I tell you."

•   •   •

By the time they went down to the lobby he had gone over his plan five times. It wasn't much of a plan, really. They were simply going to go out the back way and then come up on the men from two different positions.

He'd pounded into her head the importance of getting the men in a cross fire without hitting each other with errant shots.

"Now, do you understand—" he started to say in the lobby.

"I've got it, Clint," she said. "I understand the concept of a diagonal line of fire."

"All right," he said. "Let's find the back door."

They went up and asked the clerk and he said, "There ain't one."

"No back door in the whole place?" Clint asked, wondering if they were going to have to climb out a window.

"Not for the guests."

"What about for the employees?"

"Well, there's one through the kitchen, but you can't—hey!"

They weren't listening. They were already heading through the dining room to the kitchen.

"I'm sorry—" a waiter started to tell them, but they breezed past him as well and entered the kitchen.

"Hey!" a cook yelled as they brushed past him.

"Here," Clint said, finding the back door. He opened it and let Esther go out ahead of him.

"Okay," he said, when they were behind the building. "I'll go around to the right, you take the left."

"What do we do if they see us?"

"If they see you, you better shoot before they do."

"Right."

He could see from the look on her face that she was frightened. He didn't say anything about it, though.

"Good luck," he said instead. "See you when it's all over."

"I hope so," she said.

Clint watched as she moved along the back of the building until she found an alley and disappeared into it. He moved to his right then, looking for an alley of his own.

When he reached the mouth of the alley he peered around and saw the four men still standing across from the hotel. He slid from the alley, keeping his back pressed against the storefronts, and worked his way halfway down the block before chancing a sprint to the other side. He made it without being seen and got himself into position behind some barrels where he could watch the men and look for Esther at the same time.

Now all he had to do was wait.

Esther Hayes thought about what she had told Clint Adams about living on borrowed time. Did that mean that she had to throw it away? Why couldn't she just go on with her life and get as far away from Horizon as possible?

It was the dreams.

She dreamed every night about having that rope around her neck, about how it felt when the horse ran out from under her and the noose tightened.

She knew there was only one way to get rid of the

dreams, and that was to make the men who were responsible for them pay—and that included Brian Wesley. He had to shoulder most of the responsibility, even though he wasn't there when they actually hanged her.

She reached the mouth of her alley and peered out. She could see the men, and then she could see what they couldn't as Clint ran across the street. Could she also make it without being seen? Or would they spot her and start shooting at her?

As scared as she was, she knew there was only one way to find out.

She watched the men closely, and when they all seemed to be staring at the front door she stepped out and started across the street.

FORTY

Sheriff Kincaid came out of his office and saw the woman running across the street. It was obvious from the way she ran that she was trying not to be seen. He recognized her immediately as Esther Hayes and wondered what the hell was going on.

That was when he saw the four men stationed across the street from the hotel.

When he recognized Ted Shelton among the four men, he knew what was going on. He wasn't the smartest man in the world, but he could figure this out. Shelton and his friends were waiting for Adams and the woman to come out of the hotel. What they didn't know was that she was already out, and Adams probably was, too.

There was going to be some shooting on the street pretty soon, and he didn't want any part of it. He decided to go into his office, wait for the shooting to begin and end, and then come out and see what the results were.

After all, that was his job, wasn't it?

Clint saw Esther finally make her run across the street, successfully. For a few moments he had wondered if she would be too frightened to make it, but now she was on the same side of the street as him and the four bush-whackers, and it was time to make a move.

He started down the street, keeping close to the store-fronts as he had before, only this time, on the same side of the street, there was less chance of being seen.

He just had to get close enough to make the first move, and he hoped Esther had the patience to wait.

Ted Shelton was about out of patience, as were the men standing with him. Still, it was early and it was possible that Adams and the woman were still in bed.

Shelton remembered the feel of the woman's breast in his hand just before they hanged her. She was a slim woman, and he'd wished he had some time to sample the rest of her before they killed her. It was a shame to kill a woman who looked like that, but he had been paid a lot of money to see that it got done.

Now he had to do it again, and he wasn't being paid extra for it. Too bad he couldn't take some time with her this go around, but there just wasn't any. Besides, she had a man with her this time, and there were only four of them instead of seven. He didn't know who the man was, but they had all decided that he would be taken out first, before the woman. If they did that, maybe there *would* be some time to have some fun with the woman

before killing her. He knew that Parnell and the others—
Haywood and Lester—wouldn't have minded either.
They'd all talked about what a fine-looking woman
she'd been after they killed her—the first time, that is.

This second time there were going to be no mistakes.

Esther moved closer to the four men just a few feet
at a time, moving with the elaborate care of someone
who is doing something for the first time. She wasn't
sure how close to get, and she wasn't sure what to do
when she got there. She was going to have to wait for
Clint to make the first move, but she was also going to
have to be in position to help him when he did.

She did not want to let Clint down. He'd done so
much for her already, and here he was risking his life
for her again.

If he died because of her, she'd wish she had died at
the end of that rope after all.

FORTY-ONE

Back on the Triple-9 ranch Brian Wesley was having breakfast with his wife Denise. They hadn't spoken last night when he got home, so this was the first time they were seeing each other since he'd sent her home from town.

They had a cook, so Denise had not been at the table when he first came down and started eating.

"Nice of you to wait for me," she said when she did come down.

"Didn't know when you were getting up," he said.

She sat down and the cook, a Mexican named Sanchez who had been cooking for them for three years, brought out her breakfast, set it in front of her, and scurried away. He did not want to be in the room when the *patron* and his wife started yelling at each other.

"Do you want to tell me what happened yesterday?" she asked.

"Not really."

"Brian—"

Wesley put his fork down and glared across the table at her. In the early days of their marriage that glare had been enough to silence her, but lately she had taken to simply glaring back.

"Denise, I wish you wouldn't start putting your nose in my business."

"I think Esther Hayes being back in town is my business, Brian."

"Esther Hayes doesn't mean anything to me now. She never meant anything to me."

"I hope not," Denise said. "God, I'd hate to think you could have done what you did to her if she meant something to you."

"What are you talking about?" He picked up his fork again.

"My God, Brian, you had her hanged."

"I did no such thing," he said. "Whatever posse or group of bounty hunters who had taken off after her obviously got too carried away."

"And hanged an innocent woman."

"She was not innocent."

"She wasn't guilty of murder."

"She was guilty of getting in my way," Wesley said. "I'm launching my political campaign next year, Denise. Do you think I could have her popping up, claiming—"

He stopped short and she frowned.

"Claiming what, Brian?"

"Never mind."

"Claiming what?" Denise asked again. "What could

she have possibly done to threaten your career?''

''Nothing.''

Denise stared at her husband for a few moments, and then something came to mind.

''Oh, dear God.''

''Denise,'' Wesley said, ''don't jump to conclusions.''

''Good God,'' Denise said, ''she's pregnant, isn't she?''

''Denise—''

''You not only hanged a woman, you hanged a woman who is pregnant with your child.''

''Denise—'' he said again.

She was staring at him differently now as she rose from the table.

''What kind of monster—''

He cut her short by smashing his fist down on the table, and then getting out of his chair and around the table so fast that she barely had time to move before he grabbed her by the shoulders.

''Denise, shut up! You don't know what you're talking about.''

She stood stiffly in his grasp and stared up at him.

''I know one thing,'' she said.

''What's that?''

''I'd better not become a threat to you,'' she said. ''God knows what you would do to me.''

He stared at her for a few moments, then released his hold on her.

''You know what, Denise?'' he said, much more calm. ''It'd probably be a good idea if you kept that in mind.''

FORTY-TWO

No matter what position he tried, Clint could not see all four men clearly. He doubted that Esther could see all four either. However, if she was able to see just one—specifically the one he *couldn't* see—then they should be able to make this work.

There was only one way to find out.

He drew his gun and stepped out slightly into the open.

"You fellas want to stand fast," he called out. "You're covered from both sides."

The three men he could see stiffened and froze at the sound of his voice.

"Who's in charge?" Clint asked.

"Don't know what you're talkin' about, mister," the man closest to Clint said. "We're just standin' around."

"You're waiting for me to come out the front of the hotel," Clint said. "Instead, I came out the back. You're wait is over anyway, though."

The man gestured, spreading his arms away from his body in a shrug.

"Still don't know what you mean, friend—"

"You're covered on both sides, like I said," Clint said, cutting him off. "Drop your gun belts."

"Don't know if we want to do that, friend," the man said. "You might shoot us anyway, you and your . . . friend."

"You're right," Clint answered, "we might. That's a chance you're going to have to take."

"There's another chance we could take."

"What's that?"

"We could go for our guns," he said. "There's four of us and two of you."

"How do you know there's two of us?" Clint asked.

The man hesitated, then said, "You said—"

"I said you were covered from both sides. I didn't say how many of us there were. The only way you could know that is if you knew it ahead of time. You knew how many people you were waiting for to come out of the hotel."

The man didn't respond.

"Still want to play innocent?" Clint asked.

"Parnell," the man called out.

"Yeah?"

"What do you see on your side?"

There was a moment's hesitation, and then a man called out, "The girl."

"That's all?"

"That's it."

Slowly, the man turned his head to look at Clint.

"Just you and the girl, friend?"

"That's it," Clint said.

"Think you can take us?"

"There's only one way to find out," Clint said, "isn't there?"

Clint's eyes and the eyes of Ted Shelton locked.

"What's your name?"

"You don't know?" Clint asked.

"No, I don't."

"Wesley didn't tell you?"

"No," Shelton said, "he just said the girl had a man with her."

"Does my name matter?"

"It might."

"Meaning that if you knew who I was you might just walk away from this?"

Shelton shook his head and said, "I don't know if we can do that, no matter who you are. Would you let us walk away?"

"No," Clint said.

"Why not?"

"Because you hanged a woman," Clint said. "I can't understand how someone could do that—let alone how seven men could be persuaded to do it."

"Money," Shelton said. "Money's a big persuader."

"He paid you that much money?"

Shelton shrugged.

"It was a lot to me."

"That I find even harder to forgive," Clint said, "that you did it for money."

"Money can't buy you, huh, mister?"

"No."

"What about the girl?"

"She can hear you," Clint said. "Why don't you ask her? She's the one you hanged from a tree."

Shelton laughed shortly and shook his head.

"I don't guess she came all this way to be bought off," he said.

"No."

"You ain't gonna tell us your name," Shelton asked, "before we kill you?"

"Before I kill you," Clint said, "my name is Adams, Clint Adams."

The smile on Shelton's face fell away abruptly.

"You're lyin'."

"What did he say?" another man asked. "What's his name?"

"He claims his name is Clint Adams," Shelton said.

There was silence, and then another man's voice asked, "The Gunsmith?"

Clint didn't answer.

"Hey, Ted," someone said, "nobody said nothin' about no Gunsmith."

"You can all drop your guns," Clint called out, "and we'll take you to a federal marshal."

"For what?" Shelton asked.

"For hanging an innocent woman."

"She's wanted for murder."

"Except that there wasn't any murder," Clint said. "That will make it a little hard for you to use that as a defense."

"What do we do, Ted?" one of the men called out.

"You took the money, Haywood," Shelton said. "That means you go all the way."

"But . . . he's the—"

"There are four of us and one of him," Shelton said.

"And me," Esther called out, speaking for the first time. "Don't forget this is all about me."

"I remember you, missy," Shelton said. "I remember what you feel like. You probably had my finger marks on you when you woke up from the dead, didn't you?"

Clint stared hard at the man now. He was the one who had groped Esther so hard that he'd left bruise marks on her breast.

"Enough talk," Clint said. "You men have a choice. Drop the guns, or go for them."

"Ted—" a man's voice said tentatively.

"No choice, Lester," Ted Shelton called out, "we got no choice."

And he drew his gun.

FORTY-THREE

Esther watched as the man closest to her drew his gun and started to turn toward her. Since she already had her gun out all she had to do was fire, but she hesitated. She remembered what Clint had said about never having fired at a man before. Thinking about that slowed her down and when she finally pulled the trigger the man had triggered his weapon also.

The bullet struck her high on the left side, in the shoulder. It spun her around, but she had already fired, and her bullet hit the man in the center of the chest.

She staggered and went down to one knee, but she managed to hold onto her weapon through the pain. There were still three more of them, and Clint would need help.

She tried to get to her feet, but she couldn't seem to move them. The pain in her shoulder was intense. She didn't think anything could be worse than being hanged, but this was. Her body felt like it was on fire, but her head felt cold.

How could that be?

Clint watched as Ted Shelton drew his gun and turned toward him.

Too slow, he thought as he drew his own weapon, too damned slow.

He shot the man in the chest before he could fire his weapon. A shocked look came over Shelton's face. His gun fell from his hand, and then he fell forward, landing on it.

Clint stepped out further and had a good, clear view of the second man. Instead of turning toward Clint, the man was ducking for cover. Clint fired a second too slow—getting old?—and the man disappeared behind a horse trough.

The third man, Haywood, made a fatal mistake. He turned toward the woman and saw his partner, Parnell, shoot her. He saw the bullet hit, and then he turned away, toward Clint. By this time Lester had ducked for cover and Haywood was out in the open. He saw Clint raise his gun and just had time to say two words—"Oh, shit"—before a bullet hammered him in the stomach and another struck him in the back and he went down.

Esther forced herself to her feet, even though she couldn't feel her legs. She saw one man run for cover while the other was turning toward Clint. She fired once, hitting the man in the back, and watched him fall. With him out of her line of sight she saw Clint standing there, holding his gun, and then she went to her knees again.

Clint saw Esther, knew she had hit the man with a shot also. He also saw the blood on her and knew she was hit. As she went to her knees, he kept himself from running to her. There was still one man left.

The first man—Shelton—had called out the others' names, but Clint couldn't figure out who was left.

"You're all alone, friend," he called out. "Toss out your gun."

"Will you let me go?"

"You'll go to jail," Clint said, "but at least you'll be alive."

There was no answer.

"Come on, you're outgunned now two to one. The odds are very different and not worth playing."

After another moment the man called out, "Okay, okay, I'm comin' out. Hold your fire. Here's my gun."

The gun came flying out and landed in the dirt, then the man stood up with his hands in the air.

"Get on the ground and sit on your hands."

"Wha—"

"Do it now!"

The man dropped to the ground and sat on his hands, hoping that he wasn't going to be shot in that position.

Clint kept the man covered and walked over to Esther.

"Esther, can you hear me?"

She was on her knees, her hands dangling at her sides. He could see where the blood was coming from, a wound in her shoulder.

"I can't feel my legs."

"I know."

"I'm hot and cold."

"You're in shock," he said. "We'll get you to a doctor and you'll be fine."

"Did we get them?"

"Yes, we got them."

Clint turned when he heard footsteps and found himself looking into the face of Sheriff Amos Kincaid. The man threw up his hands, showing that they were empty.

"You're a little late, Sheriff," Clint said, "or are you?"

"Huh? Uh, what's goin' on?"

"Like you didn't know," Clint said.

"Adams—"

"Never mind. Take that man over to the jail and lock him up. If I don't find him there later you'll have to answer to me."

"A-are you tellin' me how to do my—"

"Yes, I am. Where's the doctor?"

"Down the street. He's got a big shingle hanging out next to the dress shop."

"I'm taking Miss Hayes over there. I'll be checking on the prisoner, and then I'll be sending for a federal marshal."

The sheriff didn't know what to do with that.

"You better get the street cleaned off, too," Clint said, helping Esther to her feet. "Your citizens might not like waking up to a mess."

FORTY-FOUR

The doctor was able to get the bullet out of Esther's shoulder without any problem and announced that she would need some rest but that she'd be fit.

"Thanks, Doc," Clint said.

They were in his outer office while Esther was lying in his examination room.

"I couldn't help noticing the scar on her neck. Is that from a rope?"

"It is."

"Nasty thing. What happened?"

The doctor's name was Carr, and he appeared to be in his sixties. Clint wondered how long the man had lived in Horizon and how well he knew Brian Wesley.

"She was hanged by a lynch party."

"Jesus! They hanged a woman?"

"That's right."

"Animals. I hope they get what's coming to them."

"They have, most of them. There are only two left."

"Who are they?"

"One I don't know, but the other one's name is Brian Wesley."

"Wesley was with that party?" the man asked, aghast.

"No, but it was his idea. He was smart enough to stay home."

"B-but why would he have that done to her?"

"You don't know, Doc?"

"Why should I?"

"Are you friends with Wesley, Doc?"

The doctor frowned.

"If I was, and I knew about what he'd done, do you think the young lady would have survived her bullet wound?"

"I hope so, Doc."

The doctor seemed offended, which suited Clint just fine.

"I am not now nor have I ever been friends with Brian Wesley," Carr said. "We sit on the town council together, and I think he is . . . reprehensible."

"Do you know anything about his desire to go into politics?"

"I believe he is launching a campaign next year."

"For what office?"

"Governor."

"Can I take her to the hotel now?" Clint asked.

"Not now," the doctor said. "Let her get some rest first. In her condition, I think she'll need more time to recover."

"Her condition?" Clint asked. "What condition is that?"

"You don't know?"

"Know what, Doctor?"

"The young lady is pregnant."

Clint stared at the man, stunned.

"No, I didn't know."

"Am I to understand," the doctor asked, "that this unborn child is Brian Wesley's?"

"It would explain a lot, wouldn't it, Doc? Like why he'd want her dead instead of just gone."

"Hmm," Dr. Carr said, "a man like that's not fit to walk the streets, let alone be governor."

"I couldn't agree more," Clint said.

Clint left Esther in the care of the doctor and went over to the sheriff's office.

"He's in a cell," Kincaid said as soon as Clint entered.

"Good."

He bypassed the sheriff and walked into the back. The man in the cell was lying on a cot staring at the ceiling.

"What's your name?" Clint asked.

"Lester," the man said without moving.

"Who's left?" Clint asked.

"I don't know—"

"Come on, come on, the time for lying is past," Clint said. "There's one left. Who is it?"

"Ollie," the man said, "Ollie Grant."

"Where is he?"

"I dunno," he said. "Shelton said he was paid off by Jawbone and he left town."

"What part did he have in the hanging?"

"He was just there."

"Who put the rope around her neck?"

"That was Ted, Ted Shelton."

"And who slapped the horse from beneath her?"

"That was Haywood."

"What did you do?"

Now the man looked at him.

"The truth is, mister, I tracked her, but I didn't want her hanged."

"But you didn't stop it."

"No," the man said, looking back at the ceiling, "I didn't."

Clint stood there staring at the man for a few moments.

"Mister," the man said finally, "I'll say whatever you want me to say. I'll tell a judge that Brian Wesley paid us to track her and hang her, if that's what you want."

"I might need you to do that," Clint said, "if I don't kill Wesley first."

FORTY-FIVE

Clint rode out to the Triple-9, knowing that he was taking a chance going alone, but he didn't have much choice. There was absolutely no one in town he could have taken with him to back him up.

He knew he could have sent for a federal marshal, but that would have taken too long, and he was too angry about Esther to wait. He'd thought Brian Wesley was a monster to have a woman hanged, but a woman who was carrying his baby? That was going too far.

As he rode up to the house he saw the big-jawed man walking to the house from the barn. Jawbone saw him at the same time and quickened his pace. As he passed two ranch hands he said something to them and they fell into step with him. None of the three of them were armed.

They all reached the house at the same time, and Clint didn't bother to dismount yet.

"What do you want?" Jawbone asked.

"I want your boss."

"He can't talk to you now," Jawbone said. "You're supposed to meet him tonight—"

"I don't want to wait until tonight," Clint said, "and besides, I didn't say I wanted to talk to him, I said I wanted him."

Jawbone frowned, obviously unable to appreciate the difference.

"You better turn around and ride out," he said. He and the hands blocked his path to the stairs that led to the front door.

"Or what?" Clint asked.

"We'll put you off Wesley land," the big man said.

Clint drew his gun and asked, "With what?"

The ranch hands looked nervously at Jawbone, who was standing between them.

"You wouldn't shoot unarmed men," Jawbone said.

The men on either side of him hoped that he was right.

"Okay," Clint said, "then I won't."

He kicked Duke in the sides and the big gelding leapt forward. The two ranch hands leapt out of the way in time, but Duke ran right into Jawbone, knocking him down. Horse and rider went up the steps, and Duke never stopped. He rammed the door and it flew open and off its hinges, and ended up lying flat on the floor in the house.

"What the hell—" Denise Wesley shouted, but she stopped when she saw Clint. She was halfway down the stairs from the second floor.

"Where is he?"

"How dare you—"

"Never mind that, Mrs. Wesley," Clint said, still mounted. "Where is your husband?"

"Get that horse out of my house."

"Mrs. Wesley, your husband tried to have me and Esther Hayes killed today. Now if your outrage yesterday at hearing that he had her hanged was real, you'll be just as outraged to find out that she is pregnant."

The indignation drained out of Denise Wesley's face and her shoulders slumped. She looked suddenly ill.

"Now where is he?"

"You said . . . he tried to have you killed today?"

"He had four men try to bushwhack us outside our hotel this morning—four of the same men who hanged her."

"Is she . . ."

"She's not dead. She's hurt, though, and I had to take her to the doctor. He told me she's pregnant."

Denise sank onto a step.

"Denise," Clint said, in a softer tone, "where is he?"

"He's—he's in his office." She pointed. "Down that hall."

"Thank you. You better go upstairs now. I suspect Jawbone will be back here any minute with some armed men. You'll be safer upstairs."

She nodded. Clint dismounted and led Duke into the living room, where he left him.

As he started down the hall he said to Denise, "I'm sorry about the horse."

FORTY-SIX

He walked down the hall until he saw a closed door
at the end. There were no other doors along the way.
He walked to the door and then flattened himself against
the wall next to it.

"Wesley?" he shouted. "It's Clint Adams. I'm coming in."

Four shots splintered the door even before he had
stopped speaking. Wesley obviously had heard the com-
motion outside and was ready for him—or so he
thought.

Wesley was inexperienced at this sort of thing. Clint
figured the man would just assume that he'd hit him by
firing through the door. Clint kicked the door open and
went in low, his gun held out in front of him. He rolled
through the door, came up on his knees, and took only
a split second to locate Wesley and train his gun on him.

Wesley, taken by surprise, was actually still pointing
his gun at the door.

"Put the gun down," Clint said.

Wesley didn't comply. He was looking at Clint, his eyes wide with surprise.

"Don't make me kill you, Wesley," Clint said. "Drop it on the floor in front of the desk."

Wesley hesitated just a few more seconds before leaning forward slightly and dropping the gun.

"You'll never get out of here," he said, finding his voice. "My men will be outside waiting for you. They'll cut you down."

"If they do," Clint said, "you won't be alive to see it."

Clint knew that men with big plans for the future were afraid to die, and Wesley was no exception.

"No, wait, wait," Wesley said, putting his hands out in front of him.

"Wait for what?"

"We can make a deal."

"Are you going to offer me money again?"

"There's got to be some amount you'll take," Wesley said.

"No," Clint said, "there isn't."

"Wait! Don't kill me!"

"Why not?"

"I—I—take me into town. Turn me over to the sheriff."

"For what? I have no proof that you did anything."

"I—I'll confess."

"To what?"

"Uh—to anything you want."

"You had Esther framed for murder?"

"Yes."

"And then you had her hanged?"

"Yes."

"Even though you knew she was pregnant."

Wesley stammered but it was clear from his eyes he'd known.

"Your own child, Wesley," Clint said disgustedly. "I think you can kiss the governor's mansion good-bye."

"W-what?"

"It's all over," Clint said.

"You're gonna kill me?"

"I'm going to take you to town and put you in a cell, and then we'll wait for a federal marshal to arrive. We'll tell him our stories and see what happens."

"He'll believe me."

"I left one of your men alive this morning," Clint said. "He'll testify to everything."

"No," Wesley said, "wait, there's got to be a deal—"

"I'm taking you in," Clint said. "That's the only deal I'm making."

"Wait—no, no, wait—"

Clint suddenly became aware that the man was not talking to him. He looked at the doorway and saw Denise Wesley standing there with a gun. Her face was contorted into something ugly, and he knew she was going to shoot.

"Denise—"

"Bastard!" she shouted, and pulled the trigger—and she kept pulling it until the gun was empty.

The impact of the shots pushed Wesley back against the wall and pinned him there until, when the gun was finally empty, he slid to the floor, leaving a bloody trail on the wall behind him.

Clint didn't bother disarming Denise because she couldn't do any further harm with an empty gun. He walked around the desk to check Wesley, who was dead before he hit the floor.

He stood up and looked at Denise.

"Why?"

"Because he ruined everything, the bastard," she said. "I could have been the governor's wife, but he ruined it."

Clint just stared at her.

"I never loved him, not really," she said, "but I wanted to be the governor's wife. When you rode in, I knew it was all over."

She looked at Clint, smiled—obviously thinking about everything Wesley would be leaving behind—and said, "Then suddenly I thought how nice it would be to be his widow."

FORTY-SEVEN

Several days later Clint was sitting on Esther's bed at the hotel.

"Doctor says I can ride by the end of the week," she said. "He says I'm a fast healer."

"Well," Clint said, "we already knew that, didn't we?"

"How did you get the marshal here so fast?"

"Brian Wesley *was* going to run for governor," Clint said. "That made him sort of important. They got a man out here real quick. Lester, the fella in jail, told him everything."

"And what about Denise?" she asked. "What's going to happen to her?"

Clint shrugged.

"Nothing. She told the marshal she shot her husband to save me."

"But . . . she didn't."

"It doesn't matter."

"You backed up her story?"

"Why not? Let her have the house and whatever else he left behind. She did manage to get me out of the house and off the land without getting killed. Those ranch hands might have shot me dead if she hadn't ridden off with me."

"I guess you're right."

He took her hand and said, "How are you feeling, really?"

She smiled at him warmly and said, "I'm all right. What would I have done with a baby anyway—especially his baby? I would have had to explain to it what kind of father it had. It's better this way."

According to the doctor it was either the hanging that made her lose the baby or the shock of being shot, or both combined. Whatever it was, the baby was gone.

"So what are you going to do now?" he asked.

"Get on with my life, I suppose. Are you riding out today?"

He nodded.

"It's time for me to go."

She pulled him to her and kissed him.

"Thank you," she whispered, "for everything."

He squeezed her hand and said, "Take care of yourself, Esther."

"We'll see each other again," she assured him.

"I'd like that," he said.

He got up and left the room. She knew he had Duke downstairs in front of the hotel, waiting for him. She also knew that she still had one thing left to do.

There was a man out there named Ollie Grant who thought he'd gotten away scot-free.

Watch for

JERSEY LILY

173rd novel in the exciting GUNSMITH series
from Jove

Coming in May!